Swiftwagon

Also by Gordon D. Shirreffs

Mystery of Lost Canyon

They Met Danger

Swiftwagon

Gordon D. Shirreffs

WOLFPACK
PUBLISHING
— EST 2013 —

Swiftwagon

Chapter One

THE SUN WAS LOW OVER THE WESTERN HILLS, but the heat of the day still clung like a thick woolen blanket about Caballo stagecoach swing station. Young Alec King stood beyond the station gate, looking south along the rutted road that crossed Caballo Wash and then swung upward in a long, lazy curve, finally disappearing into the hazy hills. Mike Tagger's Concord stagecoach was overdue at the swing station for its change of horses. There wasn't even a thread of dust to mark the swift passage of the vehicle through the hills. In all the vast expanse of desert and mountains, there was no sign of life. There seemed to be an ominous air about the silent land.

Lije Parsons, the station manager, came out of the low main building and crossed the quadrangle of hard-packed earth to stop beside Alec. He shoved back his battered hat and mopped his red face with his bandanna. "Any sign of the coach yet, Son?" he asked Alec.

Alec shook his head. "Mike is an hour late, Lije."

Lije was worried. He scratched in his thick black beard. "Ain't like Mike to be late. Mebbe a broken wheel or thoroughbrace, you think?"

Alec shrugged. It was a lonely twenty miles from Yavapai Wells, the division station on the Butterfield Stagecoach Line. That was where Alec's father's branch line made a junction with the great Butterfield Stagecoach Line. Mike was one of the best stagecoach drivers on the King Stagecoach Line, and he made it a point of honor never to be late.

Miguel Estrada, the head hostler in charge of the stagecoach teams, came out to the gate. He studied the empty road through narrowed eyes. "There is no sign yet?" he asked in his soft voice.

Lije shook his head. "He's had trouble, I'll warrant. I been expecting it. Our coaches are getting plumb rickety. Like I said to Alec here: 'Mebbe a broken wheel or thoroughbrace.'"

Miguel leaned against a gatepost. "*Los indios,*" he said quietly. "The Apaches."

Lije paled. "We ain't had any trouble with them for a long time."

"That does not matter, *amigo*. We are so isolated here it is easy for them to strike like the rattlesnake and then disappear like wind-driven smoke."

Alec looked up at the somber hills. "There is no smoke in the hills," he said.

The two men looked at each other. They had seen Apache raids in past years. They had generally been forecast by the smoke of burning ranch houses in the distant hills. The high adobe wall of the station and its corral bore many a bullet and arrow pockmark. There were holes in the thick wooden gates, where Alec had patiently dug out bullet slugs and flint or steel arrowheads—mementos of past attacks.

Alec walked back into the quadrangle. The fresh team of six horses stood near the corral. Swing stations had no facilities for feeding passengers. Their only function was to supply fresh relays of horses for the stagecoaches. Alec walked into the corral. Biscuits, his pony, trotted to him and nuzzled his shoulder roughly. Alec grinned as he saddled the pony. Biscuits was always ready for a brisk run along the road. He led the pony to the main building and then went in to get his weapons. He brought out his battered Sharps single-shot carbine and slid it into the figured leather scabbard that Miguel had made for the weapon.

Alec twirled the cylinder of the little Wells Fargo Colt his father had given him before he had left the home station of Yucca Flats to work at Caballo swing station. "You might never need it. Son," Bert King had quietly said, "but always keep it close at hand."

Alec sheathed the Colt and then led Biscuits to the gate.

Lije turned to look at Alec. "No riding, Son," he said firmly.

Alec shook his head. "It's not for pleasure, Lije. I'm going to look for Mike."

"No!"

"He is safe enough if he does not go into the hills," said Manuel. "Let him go. Lije."

Lije looked puzzled. It was a lot of responsibility having a fifteen-year-old boy at his station, and particularly the son of the stage line owner, but Alec was like his father, and once he had made up his mind, there wasn't much Lije could do about it.

"Ride to Antelope Cone," said Lije. "You can see three or four miles into the pass from there. But don't you go no farther! You understand. Alec?"

Alec nodded as he mounted Biscuits. He kneed the little sorrel to pass the two men and then touched him lightly with his heels. Biscuits danced about as he headed down the road. Alec had been so busy with his station duties that he hadn't had much of a chance to ride out of late.

He looked back at the station as he crossed the pebbly wash. The two men were watching him. Pete Gallery, a hostler, joined them as he watched. He held a long rifle in his hands.

Alec let Biscuits run free beyond the wash. A chaparral cock scuttled out of the mesquite brush and ran awkwardly but swiftly ahead of the pony, carrying a squirming lizard in his long beak. A hawk floated high overhead like a scrap of charred paper. Alec grinned, despite his worry about Mike Tagger. The hawk was after the lizard, too. The hawk drifted down until he was just above the road runner, but the cock was too smart for the hawk and he darted into the brush and disappeared from sight. The hawk veered off toward the low sand hills.

Alec patted Biscuits. It was good to be away from the station for a time. In the three months he had worked there, he had worked his way up from the lowest greaseboy to assistant hostler. His paycheck had come through as regularly as those of the other station employees. It was Bert King's way. He paid a man for what he did, and as far as he was concerned, his young son was doing a man's work. But Alec wanted to drive a stagecoach—to become a regular "whip" on the King Stagecoach Line. Every chance he got, he rode with young Dance Birney, one of the upcoming drivers in that part of Arizona Territory. Alec was learning how to handle the six-horse, loosely hitched Concord team. Four times now, Dance had allowed Alec to drive a team over part of the way between Caballo swing station and the junction at Yavapai Wells, and then over part of the way back to Caballo station. Dance, as young as he was, barely twenty, was a thorough and exacting teacher.

Antelope Cone loomed up through the plum-colored haze. Sand swirled up from the flats and scurried through the brush, only to disappear from sight. But there was still no sign of dust on the stage road.

The sun was almost gone when Alec urged Biscuits up the easy lower slope of Antelope Cone. Alec dismounted near the top and ground-reined the little sorrel. He took his carbine and slogged his way up the last difficult stretch. Alec stood up on a boulder and scanned the road. There was no stagecoach in sight. He studied the shadowy notch of Owl Pass. Alec felt as if something alien was in there. Then he saw a thread of smoke wavering slowly upward. A chill of fear passed through his body. The smoke might be from the campfire of some desert rat, or maybe some careless traveler had dropped a cigar in the tinder-dry brush along the road.

"Maybe Apaches are camped in there," said Alec aloud. He looked back over his shoulder as he spoke, as if to conjure up skulking warriors, but the only living thing in sight was Biscuits.

Alec walked back to the pony, mounted him, and rode down toward the road. It was getting late, and he should turn back to the station, but something made him ride on toward the pass. He constantly scanned the brushy flats as he rode along, for a man who was not alert in that country might not live long.

His nerve held out until he reached the first defile of the deeply shadowed pass. The wind came to meet him, moaning softly as if to warn him of something unseen and dangerous in the pass. He drew out his carbine and half-cocked the hammer, placing a percussion cap on the nipple. He had been taught to shoot by Ed Schmidt, head blacksmith in the King Line shops at Yucca Flats. Ed had been one of Berdan's First United States Sharpshooters during the Civil War, and no one had ever beaten him in the turkey shoots and rifle matches held in Yucca Flats. Alec had never fired at anything but targets and an occasional deer.

The wind increased, and the smell of smoke came to Alec, mingled with the stench of charred leather and scorched varnish. The odor grew stronger as he progressed cautiously into the pass. Suddenly, a horse neighed shrilly from the darkness ahead. Alec drew rein and raised his carbine. He waited, straining his eyes against the darkness.

Biscuits whinnied softly. Alec rode on for fifty yards and then dismounted. He led Biscuits into the brush and tethered him. Working his way along the side of the pass, he placed each foot with caution on the crumbly ground.

Then he made out the Concord, standing at one side of the road. Smoke drifted up from the rear boot, or luggage compartment. The team stood patiently in harness. There was no sign of man about the coach. Alec sank down into the brush and studied the Concord. Then he scanned the brushy slopes on the far side of the pass. An owl hooted mournfully as he watched.

Alec eased down the slope until he was a hundred feet from the stagecoach. There was still no sign of Mike or any passengers. Alec walked quickly to the coach and pulled aside the canvas flap that covered the rear boot. A fire had blazed up in there and then had died away, leaving a few embers. Alec unhooked his canteen and poured water over the embers. Something rolled under his left foot as he stepped back to avoid the steam rising from the boot. He picked up a peculiar brass cartridge case. He had never seen one quite like it. He slipped it into a shirt pocket and then continued his search.

Two mailbags lay to one side of the road. The thick leather had been slashed open on both bags. Letters were scattered about them. Alec gathered them up and put them into one of the bags. He threw the bags into the front boot.

Alec froze as he heard a faint moaning noise, quite different from that of the night wind. His heart thudded against his ribs. He stood there, with trigger finger drawing up the slack of the trigger.

The moaning sound came to him again. He gathered up what little nerve he had left and passed in front of the lead horses of the team. One of the horses nuzzled him as he passed, as if glad to see him.

A scrabbling noise came from the brush. Alec looked down to see a man lying face downward, with clawed fingers raking the ground. Alec leaned his carbine against a boulder and knelt beside the man. He rolled him over. It was Mike Tagger. Blood stained the left side of his head. Mike opened his eyes, smiled faintly at Alec, then closed his eyes again.

"Mike," said Alec, "are you hit bad?"

Mike opened his eyes. "Just a crease, Alec."

"What happened?"

"Taches."

The hated name sent a quiver of fear and revulsion through Alec's tense body. He had an impulse to run to his pony and race out of the fear-haunted pass.

"Where are the passengers?" asked Alec. He lifted Mike's head as gently as he could.

"Weren't none...it was just a mail...run."

Alec helped the big man to his feet and to the coach. Mike swayed as he clambered into the coach. "Get the mail if there's any of it lying around," he said.

Alec nodded. "I got it. Two bags?"

"Yeh."

Cold sweat soaked through the sides of Alec's shirt as he closed the coach door. He looked up and down the dark pass. The moon had not risen yet. Alec got Biscuits and tethered him to the rear of the Concord. He checked the team. He talked softly to the horses as he ran his hands over the harness to see if it had been damaged. Nothing had been disturbed. He walked around the coach to check the great leather thorough-braces that cradled the boat-shaped body of the Concord. They were okay. Alec ran a questing hand over all four wheels. They were all right. Alec's inspection was part of the ritual taught to him by his father and Dance Birney.

Alec picked up Mike's hat. A buckskin bag lay near it. He picked it up and opened it. There was some kind of fine powder inside it. He held his fingers close to his eyes. They were covered with a fine yellowish substance. Lije had once told him that Apaches carried such bags, filled with *hoddentin,* the sacred pollen of the tule, which Apaches scattered about in their rites and prayers.

Alec wasted no more time. Something seemed to haunt him as he mounted to the driver's box. It stayed with him, leering through the darkness at him, waiting for him to crack. Alec took the reins and threaded them through his fingers. He took the long whip from its socket and then released the brake. He snapped the whip over the heads of the leaders. The team pulled out as if glad to get away from the brooding pass.

Alec looked back over his left shoulder. He wanted to lash the team to its highest speed, but he knew better. Dance had often told him a team must warm up to its work.

It was a harrowing ride for Alec until the sprightly leaders stepped out onto the open road beyond Owl Pass.

The coach swept past Antelope Cone, and then Alec let the team out. There was always a thrill in handling a six-horse team as if it were one unit, but this night, with a wounded man for a passenger and painted death somewhere in the darkness beyond the road, he felt as if he'd never reach Caballo swing station quickly enough.

Alec crossed the wash just as the moon began to silver the eastern hills. The Concord took the wash with a grinding of wheels, a clucking of sandboxes, and a greasy chuckling of hubs. The vehicle swayed easily on its great leather thoroughbraces as it rose up the northern bank of the wash.

Lije Parsons stood at the station gate, with a yellow pool of lantern light about him and a rifle in his big hands. He stared up at Alec. "Where's Mike?" he called out.

Alec did not answer as he drove the coach into the quadrangle and braked it to a smooth halt in a veil of fine dust. He socketed the whip, wound the reins around the brake handle, and then dropped to the ground. He opened the coach door. "Look here," he said to Lije.

Lije came close to the coach and held up his lantern. "Mike!" he said.

Mike nodded as he eased himself to the ground. The men of the station gathered around him. Pete Gallery supported the weak driver. Miguel Estrada ran to the main gate and dropped the bar into its sockets. One of the hostlers climbed up the ladder to the little watch-tower, trailing his rifle behind him.

Alec leaned against the side of the coach as Lije examined Mike's wound. There seemed to be a sudden weakness in his legs. "I saw the smoke in the pass from the top of Antelope Cone," he said. "I rode into the pass and found the coach. Mike was lying beside the road. Two mailbags had been ripped open, and the letters had been scattered about. The bags are in the front boot. I found something else, too." He handed the *hoddentin* bag to Lije.

"*Hoddentin* bag," said Lije. "Then it *was* Apaches!"

Alec nodded.

Mike wiped his forehead with a shaking hand. "They opened fire from the north side of the pass. The slug creased me. I dropped like I was dead and then rolled into the brush. I guess I passed plumb out then, because I don't remember nothing until I heard the kid moving about. It took sheer brass nerve for Alec to come in there after me, Lije."

Lije shook his head. "You was told *not* to go in there, Son."

Alec shrugged. "Dance says Apaches won't stay

near the dead. I didn't think anyone was alive in there."

"Listen to *him*," said Sam Bascomb, a hostler.

Miguel grinned. *"Muy hombre!* You are much of the man, Alec."

Lije slid a thick arm about Alec's shoulders. "Don't never do a thing like that again, Alec. Your pa would take the hide and bones off me with a whip if anything happened to you while you was under my charge."

Alec led Biscuits to the stable as Mike was carried into the station house. He unsaddled the little sorrel and then rubbed him down. He covered Biscuits with a blanket and then carried his Sharps with him as he walked out into the lamplit quadrangle. Hostlers were unhitching the coach team. Somewhere in the moonlit hills, a coyote howled mournfully.

Alec walked into the station house, where Lije was bathing Mike's head. "Lucky you got a thick *cabeza*, Mike," he was saying.

Greasy, the cook, poked his glistening bald head out of the kitchen. "You hungry, boy? I got good Mex strawberries with hot chili sauce, sowbelly, and bread pudding with lick."

Alec felt a little queasy as he thought of eating the beans and bacon. "No," he said. "Thanks just the same, Greasy. I don't feel very hungry."

Greasy drew back his head like a frightened turtle. "I know how you feel, Son, but you done a man's job, and a man has to eat after work like that."

Alec smiled. "Maybe I'd better try, Greasy." The food was easier to eat than Alec thought it would be.

When he had finished, he went into his little cube of a room and sat down on his rawhide cord bed. Then he lay down and closed his eyes. Mike was his good friend. He was always bringing Alec something from town—a new clasp knife, a bag of hard candy, a dime novel, or a magazine. Alec shuddered to think of how close the genial driver had been to death.

Chapter Two

THE MORNING HAD COME BRIGHT AND CLEAR, with no smoke staining the bright blue sky. A guard had been kept in the tower all night long, and Lije had decided to keep a lookout up there during the day, too. Alec had little to do. He looked over the damaged Concord. It would have to be hauled to the shops at Yucca Flats. But it wouldn't take much time to repair the scorched rear boot.

Alec always got a great deal of pleasure in looking over a Concord. The sun was reflected from the varnished and polished surfaces of the coach. Concords were made by the Abbott-Downing Company of Concord, New Hampshire. Skilled Yankee craftsmen had put more than just labor into making the fine vehicles, they had put part of their souls into them as well. The decking and panels were made of the clearest poplar wood. The frame was of tough ash. The wheels were also of ash, carefully weighed and balanced by hand, fitted to rim and hub as snugly as it was humanly possible to do. The manifold thorough-braces were made of the thickest steer hide. The thoroughbraces suspended the graceful boat-shaped body. There was scarcely a straight line in the entire body of the swift vehicle. The ironwork of the coach was always made from the finest Norwegian metal.

Alec walked around the coach, passing a loving hand over the smooth surfaces. The day would come when he would drive one for the King Stagecoach Line.

Alec walked out behind the thick-walled station house for his daily practice. He drove six stakes into the soft sandy soil and then tied a line to each of them. He arranged the lines through his fingers as though they were reins. Patiently, he began his practice. Dance had taught Alec how to do it. The trick was to draw back one hand, letting any one line slip while holding any two, or letting any two slip while holding one. He must practice drawing back both hands and doing likewise. In one movement of his arms, he must try to dislodge any one, two, three, four, or five stakes without disturbing any of the remaining stakes. Thus, he could telegraph his wishes to any one or more of the six horses of a coach team. It wasn't easy.

Alec practiced for an hour, trying to forget his experience of the night before. The southbound Concord was soon due. Alec dropped his lines and walked to the big gate. Sam Bascomb was doing his guard stint in the tower. Alec climbed up the ladder and stood beside Sam. They looked out across the bright desert. The sun was reflected from shiny particles in the yellowish sand. The heat of the day was already beginning to be felt. The very air seemed to shimmer and dance.

Sam rubbed his jaw. "Looking for Dance, Alec?" he asked.

"Yes."

"He ain't due yet."

"He'll come through."

"Yen...to Caballo. What happens between here and Yavapai Wells?"

"Dance always gets through," said Alec stubbornly.

"Sure. Sure."

A streamer of dust suddenly appeared low on the road to the north. "See?" said Alec.

It was always a thrill to see Dance Birney tool a Concord along the open road. He was a real whip, a jehu, a born reinsman. He could handle the ribbons as though he had been born with them in gloved hands.

A cloud of saffron dust seemed to race along the road by itself, and then the faint popping of a whip drifted on the wind to the two watchers in the tower. Dance never touched a horse with his whip, but he could snap it inches above their heads.

The swiftwagon appeared, rolling and swaying behind the six racing horses, trailing a scarf of dust behind it. The thudding of the hoofs came to Alec. Then he could see Dance, sitting bolt upright in his seat, whipstock held under the thumb of his right hand, while the whip pointed straight ahead like a lance over the nightwheel horse.

Alec felt a surge of pride as he watched Dance tool the Concord up a low rise. The sun shone on his white hat, slanted back on his head, with the long, curly blond hair showing beneath the wide brim. The thrums on his buckskin coat fluttered in the wind of his swift passage. Dance stood up, spraddle-legged, with his coat fluttering about him, his whip now held crosswise across his broad chest. The Concord reached the station. Dance hauled back easily on the reins, braked to a halt, wound the reins around the brake handle, and then dropped lightly to the ground. "Yo, greasers!" he yelled. He looked up at Alec and grinned. "Howdy, whip!"

The greasers scuttled out, pots of grease and thick brushes in their dirty hands, to slake the hot hubs and axles. The hostlers trotted out a fresh team and unharnessed the sweat-lathered one. In a matter of minutes, they had harnessed the fresh team and led away the old one. Now, the Concord was ready for the final twenty-mile run to Yavapai Wells, the end of the branch line.

Alec came down the ladder. Lije had met Dance at the gate. "Dance," he was saying, "I ain't so sure you should go on."

Dance peeled off his fine gloves and worked his long, supple fingers. "And why not, Lije?"

Lije jerked a thumb back toward the station house. "Mike Tagger was ambushed in Owl Pass last evening. 'Paches. They creased him, but he managed to keep out of their sight, while they went through the coach. They ripped open the mailbags but left the letters on the road."

Dance tilted his head to one side. "Apaches? In Owl Pass?"

Lije nodded.

Dance rested a hand on Alec's shoulder. "Any passengers?" he asked Lije.

"No. It was a mail run, with some express stuff."

"Who brought him in?"

"Alec here. The bullheaded young idjit went out to look for Mike when he was overdue. I told him to go no farther than Antelope Cone. But he's a chip off the old block. He went into Owl Pass at dusk and found Mike and the coach. He helped Mike into the Concord and then drove it back here."

Dance slapped Alec on the back. "This young *hombre* will be a real whip someday."

"Yeh," said Lije dryly. "If he lives."

"Well, Lije," said Dance quietly, "I'm going on. I haven't any passengers. Just four bags of mail for the eastern Butterfield Stagecoach Line run."

Lije waved a hand. "Suit yourself. Any news about the new road to Tres Cabezas?"

Dance shook his head. "All work is stopped. Tonto Apaches raided Cactus Spring swing station and killed one man and wounded two others. They shot up Dan Packard's road-building gang and burned three of his wagons, besides running off some of his stock. Dan says he can't get the road built in time unless he gets soldiers to guard his men. The men won't work out there without protection, and you really can't blame them."

Lije glanced at Alec. "Then the boss won't be able to get his branch line through to Tres Cabezas in time to keep his mail franchise, will he?"

"It doesn't look like it now. Ross Corson offered again to buy Bert out — lock, stock, and barrel."

"*Him?*" snapped Lije. "I'll quit the line if Corson buys out Bert."

"Bert is low on funds. Our coaches are getting to be in pretty bad shape. Quite a few men have quit our line to work for Corson. We haven't had over twenty passengers in the past month."

Alec looked away. Ross Corson had money and equipment. If Alec's father didn't get the new road through in time to the mines at Tres Cabezas, he would lose his government mail franchise. There wasn't too much money to be made initially on the new run, but holding the mail franchise would allow him to take the cream of the passenger trade between Yucca Flats and Tres Cabezas when it grew in volume. But that might take months. Then, too, there was the payroll and express business, which would help out considerably once it got started.

Dance walked into the quadrangle. He looked over the Concord that Mike had brought in. Alec watched him. Dance shoved back his hat. "They didn't take any of the horses, Alec?"

"No."

"That's odd."

"What do you mean, Dance?"

Dance shrugged. "Nothing. You ready for another lesson?"

"Sure, Dance!"

Lije held up a hand. "You won't take this boy into that pass, Dance."

Dance drew on his gloves. "There won't be any Apaches in there, if that's what you're afraid of."

"How can you be sure?"

"I *know*." Dance walked out to his coach. He swung up into his seat. "Come on, kid."

Alec ran for his Sharps carbine. He came back to the coach and mounted to the shotgun messenger's seat, placing the Sharps upright between his knees. Dance took his whip and threaded the reins through his fingers. He released the brake and spoke sharply to the team. He jerked his head at Lije. "See you tomorrow. Lije."

Lije shook his head as the Concord took the wash easily and then rolled up the far bank. The team picked up speed. The Concord rolled gently on the thoroughbraces.

Dance eyed Alec. "Scared?"

"Not with you, Dance."

Dance touched up the swing horses. It was a good-matched team. Bert King always prided himself on his teams: the dainty, sprightly leaders, the bigger and more sedate swing horses and the big, steady wheelers. But the coaches were getting a little rickety, and too many of them were spending more and more time in the repair shops.

They swept past Antelope Cone and made the

long, gradual curve into Owl Pass. "Show me where it happened," said Dance.

The team was slowed to a walk and then was braked to a halt as Alec indicated the place where he had found the coach. Dance and Alec got down to look around. Dance walked slowly up and down. "Funny," he said at last.

"How so?"

Dance looked up at the brushy slopes of the pass. "Apaches fear owls. They think they speak with the voices of the newly dead who have not yet gone to the House of Spirits. That's why they stay away from here. But the owl is a bad omen."

"But they *were* here! Mike saw them. I found a bag of *hoddentin* right about where you're standing now."

Dance plucked at his lower lip. "Yeh. You find anything else?"

"No...wait a minute! Yes, I did. Here." Alec took out the peculiar brass cartridge case he had found and handed it to Dance.

Dance eyed the hull. "Odd-looking case," he said. "You know what kind it is?"

"No."

"Ed Schmidt will." Dance placed the case in his pocket. "Let's roll that swiftwagon, Alec."

Dance took the ribbons and settled himself. "You feel up to handling this team on Two-Mile Grade?"

"Can I?"

"Sure. I want you to learn braking."

They rolled through the quiet pass. Dance whistled softly as he drove, but Alec noted he had swung his bolstered Colt up onto his lean thigh for easy access.

"You don't think it was Apaches who attacked Mike?" asked Alec.

"It doesn't look like it to me."

"Then who could have done it?"

"I don't know. But whoever did attack the coach tried to make it look like Apache work, only they don't seem to know too much about our red brethren."

There was a cold feeling in Alec as they shot out of the pass to cross a rocky flat. Ahead of them stretched Two-Mile Grade, leveling down to the bottoms along Sandy Wash.

Chapter Three

ALEC TRANSMITTED HIS WISHES TO THE swiftly moving team. The grade was tricky, with many sharp curves and sudden drops. Dance always went down it, lickety-split, as if determined to dump the coach over as quickly as possible, and Alec was moving almost too fast for his newly acquired skill.

"A loosely harnessed team such as we Americans use has all kinds of advantages over a tightly strapped team," said Dance. "A tightly strapped team punishes itself against the pole. Our loosely harnessed teams swing easily, allowing each span of horses to work almost by itself."

The team flowed easily around a curve, illustrating Dance's point.

"Our dangling harnesses must look sloppy to a British coachman, but it's a necessity out here," continued Dance. "But I hear tell that Abbott-Downing is selling their good old Concords in

Canada, Australia, and Africa, where road conditions are much like ours."

Alec shot a look at Dance. Dance always said he was twenty-three years old, but Alec knew the young driver wasn't any more than twenty. But he had been driving since he was in his early teens, and even the older drivers admitted that Dance had few equals in the business.

Dance eyed Alec's hands. Alec could feel the strain now throughout his wrists and forearms as the team took the steeper grades and sharper curves. "Rest your hands on your knees if they're getting tired," he advised.

Dance looked up. "Touch the brake!" he said quickly.

Alec did so. The slight retarding motion tightened the reins.

"You see," said Dance, "the team hears the brake. It's a signal for them, and almost instantly, they feel the tightening of the bit. Not too hard, you understand, for you'll give them hard mouths, and then they're devils to handle."

The team flowed around the curves. Alec worked brake and reins as he had been taught. He was still rough, but Dance ignored it.

Dust rose at the bottom of the grade. Dance grunted. "Corson Line coach," he said.

The Corson Stagecoach Line used the same road from Yavapai Wells into Yucca Flats, but it had its own swing stations. At Yucca Flats the Corson Line turned westward on the old Fort Irland Road, thence to Crescent City, Willow Seep, Rock Springs, to end at Fort Irland. That was one reason Bert King was losing business. Ross Corson had spanking new Abbott-Downings on his Yavapai Wells-Yucca Flats division, and they made the aging King Line coaches look pretty bad in comparison.

The Corson coach slowly climbed the grade. "That's Rig Conboy up," said Dance.

Alec grinned in admiration. Dance could spot a coach many yards away and could usually tell who was driving it by the way the other driver handled his team.

"Conboy uses breechings on his wheelers," said Dance. "Sets the big horses back into them when he brakes. Most good drivers stopped using them long ago. The breeching straps were sort of an emergency equipment used in case the brake carried away. It really doesn't help much, and the weight of the coach is usually too much for them. Personally, I think breechings are just a lot of extra harness to weigh down your wheelers."

The Corson Line coach was moving faster now. The road narrowed. Alec got a little nervous. It took delicate driving to pass another coach on that road.

The gap closed between the two Concords. Conboy was lashing his struggling team. The foam-splattered horses were working too hard. Dance spat. "He'll wear them out before he reaches Owl Pass," he said disgustedly.

Conboy was plainly visible now. His broad face

glistened in the sun. He looked up the grade and said something to his shotgun messenger.

"Want me to take over, Alec?" casually asked Dance.

Alec stubbornly shook his head. Conboy had swung over a little toward the outside of the road. It was good manners for the upcoming coach to yield as much of the road as was possible to the faster down-coming coach. Alec braked a little. Then Conboy began to hog the road, riding over the invisible middle line. Alec was forced to turn his leaders up onto the narrow shoulder bordering the road. There was a high drop just alongside his right wheels. One of his leaders jerked its head as Conboy's leaders reached him. The off-leader crowded over against the nigh-leader. Gravel shot from under the wheels as the King Line coach swayed perilously over the drop. Then Conboy was even with them.

"Get over!" yelled Conboy.

There was a bumping and scraping noise as the coaches passed each other. Alec swung his leaders back onto the road. His rear wheels slewed, showering gravel down onto the sharp-edged rocks far below the road. Alec felt a little sick.

Dance looked back. There was a frosty look in his gray eyes. "One of these days," he said softly, "I'll have to give Rig Conboy a little comeuppance. You want me to take the coach into Yavapai Wells?"

"No."

Alec didn't want Dance to know how frightened he really was. But Dance leaned back in his seat and whistled softly as he looked across the bright desert far below them.

They covered the remaining miles into the Wells in good time. Alec braked to a halt in front of the warped little shack that was the company office. He got down and looked at the side of the coach. It was scarred and splintered. Dance ran a hand over the gouge. "I'll take it out of Conboy's hide when I next see him," he promised.

They took the mailbags into the office. Harry Sievert, the agent, looked up at them from his desk. "No passengers again?" he asked.

"None," said Dance.

Sievert shook his gray head. "I haven't one reservation for tomorrow either. Bert can't keep up this way much longer."

Dance peeled off his gloves. "Mike Tagger got dry-gulched in Owl Pass last evening, Harry."

"No! Apaches?"

"Maybe, but I think not."

"Mike get hurt?"

"Just a crease. Lucky there weren't any passengers in his coach. But the mail was tampered with. We're not sure yet how much of it was taken…if any."

Sievert bit his lower lip. "Fred Horton, the postal inspector, is in town. He won't like this."

Dance nodded. "I know. Come on, Alec. Let's eat."

They walked to the Western House. Everyone they passed spoke or nodded to Dance. He was well known, for he was a true son of the Territory. He had been born during an Apache attack on his father's swing station on the old Butterfield Line. He had grown up with stage-coaching in the Territory. When his father died, Dance had supported his mother and sister by working his way up from a greaser to a driver. In seven years, he had gained a wealth of information about stage-coaching, such as few older men knew.

They ate well in the Western House. Later, Dance took Alec to the warehouse of Metzger and Company. The clerk looked up as they entered. "I've got four heavy boxes for you, Dance," he said.

"*Bueno!* We'll pick them up first thing in the morning."

"Here's the bill."

Dance scanned the bill and then paid it. Alec and Dance walked out into the bright sunshine. "What's in the boxes, Dance?" asked Alec.

Dance grinned. "Something that's going to open up the new road between Yucca Flats and Tres Cabezas. I'll tell you all about it when we get to Yucca Flats."

"I've got to go back to work tomorrow at Caballo swing station."

Dance shook his head. "Your father told me to bring you back to Yucca Flats on my return run."

They watched the westbound Overland coach come in. Dance waved to the driver. "Cas Fritchie," he said to Alec. "A top whip."

"I guess you know most of the drivers," said Alec.

"Just about."

"You could get more money working for the Southern Overland," said Alec.

"Why, so I could, but I like working for Bert King."

They walked past the Corson Line office. It was much bigger than the King Line office and had just been freshly painted. Sim Anderson, the agent, leaned against the doorpost. "I've got a full passenger load for our coach in the morning, Dance," he said with a sly grin.

"Very interesting," said Dance.

"Ross Corson will double your wages if you drive for him."

"I wouldn't work for Ross Corson for *any* amount of wages."

"Better be careful what you say about Mr. Corson."

Dance grinned. "I've already told *Mr.* Corson the same thing, Anderson."

"Yeh? The King Line is dying on its wheels. When Bert King loses the mail franchise to Tres Cabezas, he'll be lucky if Corson takes over his junk-heap Concords and spavined horses."

"Sometimes you talk too much, Anderson. We've got something on the King Line you wouldn't know about working for Corson."

"So? What might that be?"

"Honesty and loyalty to a good employer."

Sim flushed. He turned into his office and kicked the door shut.

Dance laughed. "That really hit home," he said.

Alec looked up at Dance. "Do you think my father can keep on?"

Dance placed a big hand on Alec's shoulder. "With us to back him, he will, Alec. Never lose faith in your father. Bert King isn't licked by a long shot."

————

THEY PULLED out of Yavapai Wells, heading for Caballo, in the early afternoon of the day after they had arrived. Dance had attended to some business for Alec's father during the morning. Dance drove the team, and as he drove he talked about his favorite subject of stage-coaching. He spoke of James E. Birch, the man who was said to have put an empire on wheels, who, with his great friend, Frank Shaw Stevens, organized the great California Stage Company. Both men were Yankees and stagecoach drivers who had come west to Sacramento. In its heyday the California Stage Company had carried passengers daily over a distance of fifteen hundred miles, all within the State of California.

Dance spoke of Ben Holladay and many other stage-coaching greats. He had a knack of painting a vast picture with his words, and Alec, with the added thrill of being driven by an expert on a Concord up through Two-Mile Grade into Owl Pass, then down into the desert past Antelope Cone, toward Caballo, felt as if he had actually experienced some of those pioneering days.

Alec picked up his gear and said goodbye to his friends at Caballo station. In a way, he hated leaving them, but he had a feeling his father would need him more in Yucca Flats. Alec tethered Biscuits to the rear of the coach for the trip home. The men all gathered at the gate to watch Alec leave. He waved his hat as Dance drove out onto the road for the short ten-mile run to Sidewinder Well swing station. "I'm going to miss all of them," said Alec quietly.

Dance grinned. "You'll see them again, Alec. Maybe you'll be their boss someday."

"Every one of them taught me some part of the business."

"It just proves how smart your father is."

Alec looked quickly at Dance. "I never really realized it until lately."

Dance spoke sharply to his team. "He knows this business and he wants you to know it as well. There's more to it than just sitting in an office, with a tie and collar on, writing out orders and acting like the big frog in the mud puddle. Another thing: Don't ever forget that employees respect a man who knows every job in his company, from the lowest greaseboy up to the presidency. A little honest sweat gained by doing the manual laboring of stage-coaching will give you an insight into the business a lot of company owners lack.

"Always remember that you're dealing with the most independent people in the world—Americans, and we Westerners are about the most independent Americans. You ought to know that by now."

Alec smiled ruefully. "I found that out more than once at Caballo when I messed up a job. Lije and some of the others didn't spare the owner's son any more than the other employees at the station."

"But you did respect them for it?

"I didn't at first, but I learned to. They could have forgotten the mistakes I made, to stand in good with the owner's son, but they didn't for one good reason."

"So? What was that?"

Alec looked at Dance. "Because they wanted the job done right for the King Line, that's why."

Dance nodded. "You're learning, *amigo,* and you're learning fast."

Chapter Four

Yucca flats stretched out along the dry bed of Yucca Creek. Some forty or fifty ugly, false-fronted buildings of the American period intermingled with a dozen or so adobe or field-stone buildings of the Mexican period. Yellow lamplight showed through dirty windows. From somewhere along the street, there came the tinny, off-key tinkling of a piano that had seen much better days, mingled with the bawling of mules, the groaning of heavily laden wagons, and the loud talking of people. Yucca Flats was the counterpart of many such towns in Arizona Territory, living its early violent life to the full, only eventually to die away into lonely obscurity.

Some people said that Bert King had played the fool when he had established his branch stage line from the Butterfield Stagecoach Line north to Yucca Flats. But he had filled a gap that the larger line hadn't bothered with in its search for greater business. Bert King had felt as if he was doing a service for the people of the area. It was a cinch that the prospect of huge profits hadn't lured him to do his life's work in Yucca Flats. But he had always dreamed that Arizona Territory would be a great state someday, and he had wanted to play a part in the making of that state. There was a great deal of the visionary in Bert King.

Dance and Alec left their dusty coach in the stage yard and then walked down the street to the main office of the line. Alec's father sat behind his scarred desk, looking over a file of papers. He looked up at them and smiled in his easy way. Alec hadn't seen him for a month, but even in that short a time, he had changed for the worse. There were new lines etched in his lean face, and his eyes were tired.

"Happy to see you, Son," he said.

Dance dropped into a chair. "Alec will make a real whipster one of these days," he promised.

Bert King waved a hand. "I wonder if he'll ever drive for the King Line."

Dance shook his head. "Now you know I don't like to hear you talk that way, Bert."

"Let's face facts. Corson is pushing me again. The road is not being worked on. In a few weeks my mail franchise will be taken from me because I won't be able to keep up my agreement to have the Tres Cabezas run operating. My coaches are in bad shape, and I haven't got the money to keep them in repair. Now, to top it off, Mike Tagger gets ambushed, some valuable mail is stolen, and then two more drivers quit today rather than drive through Owl Pass because of what happened to Mike."

"There's still time to get the new road through."

Bert King shook his head. "Sure...if Dan Packard can get his men back on the job, but the men refuse to work without military protection. The nearest post is Fort Irland, and all they've got on duty there is a company of infantry. The cavalry is off chasing Apaches fifty miles from here."

"There still might be an answer, Bert."

"And what might that be? I'm almost at the end of my rope."

Alec studied the big map on the wall as his father and Dance talked. Bert King had blue-penciled his existing line on it, from Yavapai Wells to Yucca Flats. He had marked in red the future line to Tres Cabezas. Alec had been out in that country with his father and Dan Packard, the road-building engineer, when the new road had first been planned.

It was twenty miles to Black Rock swing station from Yucca Flats—an easy run on hard ground to the old adobe building that would serve as the swing station. From Black Rock swing station, it was fifteen miles on an easy climbing grade to Cactus Spring swing station in the Grindstone Hills. The road from Cactus Spring was narrow and winding through Pinon Pass to Stony Creek, the third swing station on the northern run. Beyond Stony Creek the going was rough indeed to Tonto Pass, the place most menaced by the tribal division of the Apaches that had given the pass its ominous name. A coach, of necessity, must move slowly in there, a natural prey for the predatory Tontos.

Tonto Pass was a home station built around an old abandoned field-stone house that was almost a small fortress. Tonto Pass home station would have facilities for meals for the passengers. The road northward from there was almost a coach driver's nightmare, with danger from ambushes, falling rocks, and washouts. The road would sweep around the base of mighty Cuchillo Peak, climb up Hogback Ridge, and then descend to Lone Hill, a planned swing station fifteen miles beyond Tonto Pass. The remaining trip, or stage, was fifteen miles into Tres Cabezas, the end of the ninety-mile northern division of the King Line.

"What about the Old Spanish Road, Bert?" asked Dance.

"Forget it. It's ten miles longer than my planned route. Full of chuckholes and covered with brush for long stretches. In places the old *camino* has disappeared entirely."

"Still," said Dance thoughtfully, "we might get a Concord through on it to keep the schedule."

"We'd need relay teams spotted along the route. We'd need herders and guards to keep the teams safe. We'd have to have forage hauled out to them, too. The costs would be excessive."

"Then it's the new road or nothing at all."

"Yes." Bert King stood up. "Dance, if you've a mind to, you can quit."

Dance stood up and shook his head. "Sometimes

you talk loco, Bert. Come on over to the stage yard. I've got something to show you."

The three of them walked up the dusty street to the big stage yard beside the shops. Some of the Concords were in the large frame shed beside the stage yard. Dance walked into the shed and placed a hand on one of the heavy boxes he had brought in from Yavapai Wells. "This might be the answer to the Tonto raids," he said quietly.

Dance loosened the thumbscrews and removed the lid of the top box. Nested in the box were heavy-looking, stubby, repeating carbines. "Spencers," said Dance. He held up one of the fine weapons. "There's a tube inside the butt stock that holds seven 56/52 caliber cartridges. You load through this butt gate you see here." He tapped the butt of the carbine.

Dance handed the carbine to Bert and then opened another box. From it, he took several heavy leather boxes. He opened the cover of one of them and showed how the box was filled with a wooden block that had been bored with ten holes. He pulled a long tin tube from one of the holes. "These tubes hold seven cartridges," he said. "A full magazine load for the Spencer. You push aside the butt gate and then pour a full load into the magazine. Saves time and fumbling around. I've brought in twelve carbines, with twelve boxes of tubes, plus enough cartridges for quite a bit of shooting if it's necessary. With these repeaters, twelve men have the firepower of a company of cavalry equipped with single-shot breechloaders."

"So?" asked Bert.

"I'd like to take eleven picked men up into the hills with me and ambush the Tontos in order to teach them a lesson. A dose of their own medicine might drive them away from the new road."

"Who paid for these?"

Dance grinned. "I saved my pay. Bert."

Bert King slapped a hard hand down on top of the nearest box. "You haven't a grain of sense, Dance!"

Dance patted a carbine. "I can spend my money any way I like, *amigo*. Besides, I like working for you, Bert. If you go out of business, I've lost the best boss I ever had."

Bert looked at Alec. "What can I do with him?" he asked helplessly.

Alec grinned. "Just do as he says, Dad."

"How about it?" urged Dance.

"I'll talk to Dan Packard. What do you plan to do?"

"Ride into the pass at night and take up a position where we can watch the new road. Packard can arm his men and then take in his wagons and gear as if he was going to start work on the road again. If the Tontos jump him, we'll jump the Tontos. Simple, isn't it?"

Bert King looked up at the roof. "*Simple,*" he says "Well?"

Bert gripped Dance's right hand. "It's a deal. I can't think of any other way to get the road through."

They walked back to the office. Alec remained outside as the two men made their plans. He raised his head as a spanking new Concord rolled by, with gilt letters on the side proclaiming to the world that it was a vehicle of the Corson Stagecoach Line.

The Concord stopped in front of the Corson stage yard. As much as Alec disliked Ross Corson he couldn't resist the temptation to look over the new Abbott-Downing.

A man stopped beside Alec as he looked over the new coach. "She's a beauty," said the man, gazing at the Concord. "Cost Ross Corson fifteen hundred dollars apiece, and he's getting in six of them. Twenty-five hundred pounds of speed there, Son. Yes, sirree!"

Alec turned away and walked to the coach shed of the King Line. A lantern hung from a beam, revealing one Concord blocked up, waiting for a new thorough-brace. Another old-timer was gathering dust and cobwebs in a corner. It had fallen into a washout, severely damaging its running gear. There were four disreputable "Celerity Wagons" at the back of the building. They were lighter than the true Abbott-Downing and used more on rough mountain roads. Parts had been stripped from them to use in the repairing of other vehicles. Off to one side, behind a partition, as if hiding from the light, was a sagging "Mudwagon" on which Alec had taken his first driving lessons. It was of no further use except as firewood.

Alec shook his head. If Ross Corson had six new Abbott-Downings coming in, he would garner all the passenger trade. The only hope left for the King Line was that Bert and Dance were a hard pair to beat in any fight, and they were far from being licked as yet.

Chapter Five

ALEC GOT UP EARLY THE MORNING AFTER HIS return to Yucca Flats. His father had met with Dance Birney and other loyal employees the night before. Alec had listened to their plans from the kitchen. It had all been settled. Dan Packard had agreed to take his men and equipment back into Tonto Pass if his men were guaranteed protection. Dance Birney was to take eleven men into the pass before Dan's arrival in order to safeguard their journey.

Alec dressed without awakening his father. He and his father lived alone in the old house, for Alec's mother had died when he was seven years old.

Alec hurried down the street to the company shops. Ed Schmidt had promised to put a better rear sight on Alec's Sharps carbine if he brought it in before regular working hours. Ed was as good as his word. He was in his little shop beside the bigger blacksmith shop. He was a broad-shouldered man with a face seemingly hewed out of mahogany. He wasn't much taller than Alec, but he was at least twice as broad. He took the Sharps from Alec's hands. "Got a fine new English Enfield rear sight I can fit on here," he said.

Alec perched on a high stool and watched Ed drive out the old rear sight with a brass punch. Ed was a top-rate blacksmith and a good gunsmith. The walls of his little shop were hung with rifles, carbines, shotguns, and pistols of many makes. Ed had carefully chosen Alec's Sharps from his collection and had presented it to him many months ago.

"Someday, I'll convert this little Sharps of yours into a brass cartridge model," said Ed.

"I'd like to have one of those new Spencers Dance Birney bought."

"Excellent repeater. But we aim to use them against the Tontos, Son. Now, maybe when we get through using them, I'll talk Dance into giving you one of them. I'll work it over for you if he does."

Dance lounged into the shop. "Morning, Ed. Morning, Alec."

Ed looked up. "You said you wanted to see me about something, Dance," he said.

Dance handed Ed the peculiar brass cartridge Alec had found in Owl Pass. "What kind of a gun would shoot one of those, Ed?"

"This is a queer one. Burnside cartridge. Worked on some of them years ago. Invented by General Ambrose Burnside. Quite a few of them were used during the war by cavalry troops. One of the first metallic cartridge carbines invented. Caliber .54."

"Looks like the primer fell out."

"No. The Burnside used an outside hammer like the Sharps." Ed reached across his bench and took a carbine from the rack. It had an unusually long breech and a big hammer. There was a second, smaller lever inside the big lever below the breech. "See here?" said Ed. "The hole in the bottom of the cartridge was left open so that the powder charge could be exploded by a percussion cap. Never had a primer, Dance. A good gun. Sturdy and more accurate than most carbines. That's why it has remained fairly popular among shooters."

"Know anyone around here who might have one?"

Ed shook his head. "Can't say that I do. I can tell you one thing, though: When you see one of them, you'll know it right enough." He operated one of the levers. The barrel tipped down like a shotgun. "Right curious operation for a breech-loading carbine."

Dance handled the weapon as if impressing it on his memory. He placed it on the rack. "How is the work coming on the coaches?"

"Slow. We've used up most of the replacement parts. I have to replace the thoroughbraces on Number Seven. Have to forge some new metal parts from stock iron. It would be easier to buy new parts, but Bert just doesn't have the money for them."

Ed finished placing the new sight on the Sharps and then handed the carbine to Alec. "You figure on doing some shooting, Alec?"

Alec shrugged. "You never know. Thanks. Ed."

Ed waved a beefy hand. "No bother. If I get time

one of these days, we'll do some target shooting together. I want you to try out the Sharps I converted to brass cartridge use."

"Thanks, Ed. I'll look forward to it."

Alec and Dance left the shop and walked down the street toward the King Line office. Alec cradled his Sharps in the crook of his left arm. Dance looked up ahead. "There's Ross Corson," he said quietly, "inspecting one of his new Concords."

Corson was a tall, dark-haired man who wore clothing a lot better than anyone else in Yucca Flats. He had a thin, arrogant nose and a personality to match it. Corson had seldom been known to carry a belt gun, but it was well known that he carried a small gun hidden somewhere on his person, and he was reputed to be able to use it with considerable skill.

Corson turned to eye Dance and Alec. "Birney," he said to Dance, "I have been waiting for some time for you to come to work on my stage line."

Dance stopped. "I'm working, Corson."

"For pennies, when you can earn dollars?"

"I'm satisfied."

Corson shrugged. He ran a hand down the shining side of his new coach. "This is the first of six new Abbott-Downings I've bought," he said with satisfaction.

Dance tilted his head to one side. "You've got enough good Concords for your two divisions."

"Yes, but not enough for *three*. Bert King won't be able to meet the deadline set for his mail franchise on the Tres Cabezas Division."

"So you figure you'll get it?"

"I can deliver the goods and mail, Birney."

Dance rubbed his lean jaw. "Seems right odd that you should think so. Apaches raid the road gangs. King has one mail coach shot up and a driver wounded. What makes you think you can do any better?"

Corson waved his slim hand. "I know I can."

"Maybe the Apaches won't be able to get any more fine repeating rifles and ammunition when you take over the Tres Cabezas run."

Corson flushed. "Just what do you mean by that remark?"

Dance leaned against the new coach. "We didn't have trouble with the Tontos for years before you drifted into this country and started competing with us."

Rig Conboy walked toward the three of them. He stopped short as he saw Dance. Dance straightened up. "Here's your ace driver Conboy, Corson. The other day, he scraped my coach while we were coming down Two-Mile Grade. Nearly drove us over the side."

Conboy spat. "The kid was driving, wasn't he? You got a nerve letting *him* drive down Two-Mile."

Dance grinned. "He's a better driver now than you'll ever be, Conboy. He doesn't need breechings on his wheelers, or a whip laid across the backs of his team, to get up Two-Mile."

Conboy's face reddened. He dropped his right hand down by his Colt and hooked a thumb over his gun belt. Dance stepped away from Alec and eyed the angry driver. "An upcoming coach, by common road courtesy, yields the right of way to a downcoming coach," said Dance quietly.

There was hate in Conboy's pale eyes. He wanted to prove he was as good a man as Dance Birney, but the cool menace in young Dance Birney's eyes held him at bay.

Ross Corson eased back out of the line of possible gunfire. He jerked his head meaningly at Rig Conboy and then slid his right hand inside his coat. Conboy shifted his feet. Men stopped to watch the two men standing in the street.

Alec had seen one gun fight outside of the Beacon in Yucca Flats. Benny Parks had been shot to death by Case Norman, one of the fastest gunmen in the Territory. Alec was scared, but his great friendship with Dance kept him rooted to the spot. He turned a little and let his carbine drop into his left hand. He cocked the big hammer. The crisp double click of the hammer warned Ross Corson. He turned to look at the muzzle of the carbine and then up at Alec's steady gaze. He backed away a little and withdrew his hand from inside his coat.

"Forget it, Rig," said Corson.

Rig slowly withdrew his hand from his belt. Then, he turned on a heel and followed his employer into the Corson Line office.

Dance turned. There was an angry look on his face. "Keep out of these things, Alec," he said.

Alec let down the hammer of his Sharps. "Corson might have got you from the back," he said quietly.

"So?" Dance smiled. "I'm sorry. Alec. Thanks."

"It was nothing. Besides, the Sharps is empty. Luckily, Corson didn't know that."

Dance slapped Alec's shoulder. "You've got nerve, kid. Facing Ross Corson down with an empty gun in your hands! We'd better not say anything to your father about this. Agreed?"

"Yes. He has enough worries as it is."

They walked to the King Line office. Dance suddenly laughed. "An empty gun. Ross Corson faced down by a fifteen-year-old kid with an empty gun in his hands."

"I'm not a kid," said Alec. "You're only five years older than I am. Dance."

Dance flushed. "*Eight* years, Alec."

Alec looked up at his friend. "Eight?"

Dance grinned. "Oh, all right. But you don't have to spread it around."

Bert King was in his office. "Shut the door," he said as Dance and Alec entered. "Sit down."

Dance and Alec sat down and looked expectantly at Alec's father.

"Well be all set tonight," said Bert King. "Dance, you'll leave about six o'clock for Tonto Pass. Ride until dawn and then go into hiding. Dan will leave here at dawn with his men and equipment. You will take Ed Schmidt. Fletch Proctor. Cass Willis, Bob Porter, Ory Carter, George Barren, Kirby Todd, Slim Pastor, Ben Richmond, Bartolome Madera, and Marty Roe. All good shots. Some of them fought in the war and most of them have Indian fighting experience."

"You'll be shorthanded, Bert," said Dance.

"What difference does that make? If the road can't be safeguarded, the King Line will fold up."

Dance nodded. He glanced at Alec. "You stay out of trouble, young'un."

Alec stood up. "I want to go along with you, Dance."

"No!" said his father.

Alec thrust out his chin. "I'm as good a shot as some of those men, and I can ride as well as any of them."

"Absolutely, but no son of mine is riding into Tonto Pass looking for a bullet to hit him in the head."

"Some other time, kid," said Dance.

Alec walked out of the office. He slammed his gun butt down on the board sidewalk, squirting the fine dust up between the planks. Suddenly, an idea hit him like an Apache arrow. He walked quickly to the company stable and got Biscuits. There was more than one way to skin a cat.

He led the sorrel to his house and tethered it in the grove behind the shed. He gathered food from the pantry and placed it in his saddlebags. Alec filled two large canteens and took a piece of tarpaulin and two blankets from a closet. He filled his pockets with cartridges and caps and took his Colt and gun belt from its hook. Alec took his gear out to the sorrel and then made a cantle pack of his blankets and tarp. He had just finished when he heard a step behind him. He turned to see the homely face of Denny Morris, the kid who lived beyond the grove.

"Hi, Alec," said Denny. "I didn't know you had come back from Caballo."

"You can see me," said Alec shortly. He had been friends with Denny for a long time, but he didn't want Denny nosing around right now.

Denny leaned against a tree. "Where are you going?"

"For a ride."

Denny grinned. "Yeh…I can see that…but where?"

Alec tightened Biscuit's girth. "Out in the hills."

"With 'Paches loose out there?"

Alec shrugged. "I won't be near Tonto Pass."

"No? I think differently."

"How so?"

Denny came closer to Alec. "Marty Roe, my uncle, came over to the house last night. I heard him talking to my stepfather. He borrowed Pa's good bay horse and his saddle. Said something about going up into Tonto Pass after 'Paches with Dance Birney and some of the men from the King Line. I heard them talking about it."

"You've got a big nose, Denny."

Denny felt his nose. "It ain't as big as yours, Alec."

Alec liked Denny better than any other kid he knew, but he didn't feel like explaining everything to him. "Well, I'll see you," he said.

Denny placed a hand on Alec's shoulder. "I missed you, Alec. You said you'd write from Caballo, but you never did."

"I was busy."

"Okay. Okay."

"You won't say anything about me going up there, will you?"

Denny flushed. "You know me better than that."

Alec swung up on Biscuits. "Yes."

Denny rubbed the sorrel's nose. "Look," he said quickly. "My pa is going to Yavapai Wells on business. My mother is visiting her sister in Tucson. I'm home alone. Why can't I go with you, Alec?"

Alec looked down at Denny. They had been together almost every day before Alec had gone to Caballo. He was ashamed because he had not written to Denny.

"I can be ready in ten minutes," said Denny.

"It might be dangerous," said Alec.

"Then you'll need me along to help you."

Alec hesitated. He wasn't even sure what he planned to do in Tonto Pass.

"I know the hills as well as you do, Alec. I can't shoot as good as you, but I can take care of myself. Besides, you promised to go camping with me when you returned."

Alec looked toward the looming Grindstone Hills to the north. It was a lonely and dangerous place, and he suddenly realized it would be fine to have Denny along for company.

"Okay, Alec?"

Alec nodded. "Get plenty of food. At least two blankets. Have you got a gun?"

Denny grinned. "Pa gave me a Sharps like yours a week ago. He said as long as you had one, I might as well have one too."

"*Bueno,* I'll meet you about half a mile north of here near the road."

Denny scuttled off through the woods.

Alec kneed the sorrel past the shed and then rode swiftly through the woods. He drew rein about half a mile from the house and dismounted to wait for Denny.

It didn't take long for Denny to appear. He rode a blocky chestnut. He waved his Sharps over his head. "Ain't it a beaut?" he yelled.

"Be quiet! Do you want to let everyone in Yucca Flats know we're out here?"

"They couldn't catch us now, Alec."

"Let's go then."

They rode through the thick brush that bordered the road until they were a good three miles from town and then they rode out on the road. Alec looked back. There was no one behind them.

Denny chuckled. "Boy," he said, "if your pa knew you were doing this, he'd skin you alive."

"What do you think you'll get when your father finds out you left too?"

Denny gulped. "I never thought of that."

"Well, don't think of it now."

A haze was forming over the hills. Alec looked up at them. There seemed to be a warning in the back of his mind, but he ignored it. It was good to be out on the open road with his friend.

Chapter Six

THE TWO BOYS COVERED THE TWENTY MILES to Black Rock swing station in good time. The route was fairly safe, for lumber wagons, driven by armed men, often came down from the hills going to the big sawmill at Yucca Flats. The boys avoided the new station at Black Rock, for Amos Ericson, the station manager, would have turned them back if he had seen them. After they passed the station, they let the horses rest, unbitted, for an hour before going on.

It was dusk when they reached Cactus Spring swing station. The two mounts were tired from their long journey. Alec drew rein as he saw the deserted station.

"You think there are any Taches around?" said Denny in a hollow voice.

"I doubt it," said Alec. "Dance says they won't stay near places of the dead, and remember the men killed in the last raid are buried near here."

"Yeh," said Denny hoarsely.

They tethered the horses in the woods nearby. The two boys walked back to the station. The blackened wood and iron of burned wagons Uttered the ground. On a knoll beyond the station were the freshly mounded graves. There was an eerie quality about the gathering darkness. Strange sounds came to them as they prowled about, and the shadows seemed to play tricks on them. A cold wind began to moan down from the hills.

When the horses were rested, they watered them and picketed them where they could graze. Denny found a good camping place under a huge rock over-hang, well shielded by brush and trees. They ate cold beef and hard biscuits and finished off half a chocolate cake Denny had brought along.

"You think we ought to take turns standing guard, Alec?" asked Denny.

Alec checked his Sharps and leaned it against the rock wall. "I don't think so. We're both dead-beat, and I doubt if either one of us could stay awake."

"You're sure those 'Paches won't come around here?"

Alec nodded. "They don't like to come around the newly buried dead."

"I ain't so sure I like being around them either."

They wrapped themselves in their blankets and tarps. "Listen to that wind," said Denny.

The wind soughed through the trees and moaned over the rocky hillside. It seemed to whisper ghoulish thoughts to Alec. He tilted his hat over his eyes and squirmed about until he found a fairly flat place to sleep. The trees swayed in the darkness. Now and then, a small nocturnal animal scuttled through the brush. Alec began to realize what fools they had been to leave the safety of Yucca Flats. He was almost tempted to go back, but the prospect of a long ride through those lonely hills was too much for him.

————

A PINON JAY chattered noisily from the junipers. The mournful cry of a dove answered the jay. "Coo-ah, coo...coo...coo..."

Alec opened his eyes. It was early morning. A uta lizard eyed him brightly from a rock and then darted agilely up the rock face to vanish into a cleft.

Alec threw back his covers and sat up. "Denny!" he called out.

Denny moaned from under his heap of covers. "It's too early, Ma."

Alec grinned. "You've got to get ready for school, dearie," he said.

Denny sat bolt upright. His reddish hair stood straight up on his head. "Jiminy," he said as he rubbed his eyes. "I thought I was still at home."

"Get out the food. I'll saddle the horses."

They worked quickly, and in twenty minutes, they were leading their mounts through the pinons and junipers until they could see the notch of Pinon Pass to the north.

"How far you figure on going?" asked Denny.

"Tonto Pass."

"That's just what I figured," said Denny dryly.

It was high noon when they watered their horses at Stony Creek. The clear, cold water rushed and gurgled about the huge boulders that had fallen in ages past from a shattered cliff hanging over the gorge. On the far side of the shallow ford was the new peeled-pole corral that had been built for the swing station. A foundation had been laid for a field-rock house.

They forded the stream and rode past the new station. A five-foot gopher snake slithered out of the road as they approached him. Here, the mountains crowded in on the narrow, winding road. A cold wind blew through the pass. The road was rough and dotted with chuckholes. Rockfalls littered it at intervals.

Denny dismounted to lead his chestnut past a bad rockfall. "Dan Packard will have his hands full getting this road ready," he said.

Alec swung down from Biscuits. "Yes, and it will take a lot of work keeping it open too."

"You think it will ever be opened to Tres Cabezas?"

"If it isn't, my dad will be out of business."

Denny nodded. "Well, I'm hoping it does go through."

They reached the first approaches to Tonto Pass in the late afternoon. The brooding mountains towered on each side of the pass. The craggy heights were stippled with juniper, pinon, scrub oak, and a few manzanitas.

"There it is," said Denny. He shivered a little in the cold wind. "What do we do now?"

Alec shoved back his hat. "Now that we're here, I'm not sure."

"Fine thing," grumbled Denny. "Ride all this way and then don't know what to do."

"You can always go back," said Alec.

Denny shook a fist at Alec. "I'm sticking," he said.

Alec smiled. "I knew you would. We'd better hole up and wait for Dance Birney and his men. Boy, old Dance is going to give me the whatfor when he finds us in here."

"I can hardly wait," said Denny.

They scouted around until they found a brushy hollow high on a slope. There was plenty of grazing. They ate and then wrapped themselves in blankets. They sat at a place where they could see the road far below them when the moon rose.

Denny whittled at a stick. "How was it at Caballo?"

"Not bad. There wasn't too much to do. It sure gets hot there, and Lije wouldn't let me leave the place very often."

"I heard you found Mike Tagger in Owl Pass and brought his coach back to Caballo."

Alec nodded.

"You see any 'Paches?"

"No, and I wasn't looking for any."

Denny eyed Alec. "You figure on working at stage-coaching when you're a man?"

"Why not? My dad has been in it since before the war."

"You sure got around, Alec."

Alec leaned back against a rock. "My father worked for the Butterfield Company before the Civil War. That was on the run between Fort Chadbourne to Emigrant Crossing in Texas. That was the year I was born. 1858. My mother didn't like the heat in Texas, so my father took a station manager's job on the Leavenworth and Pikes Peak Express. That was a good line, but it didn't last long. They ran double stages weekly through north-ern Kansas to the new town of Denver. When that line folded up, Dad went to work for the Overland Mail."

"That was a real booming line."

Alec nodded. "When the war started, my father enlisted in the Colorado Volunteers. He was in that rough march from Denver through Raton Pass in the snow to Las Vegas. Then he fought at Glorieta Pass."

"My pa was killed at Valverde," said Denny quietly.

Alec looked at his friend. Denny had never talked much about losing his father.

Denny whittled steadily. "What happened after your pa was at Glorieta Pass?"

"He was wagon master at Fort Craig. When he was mustered out, he learned that my mother had died in Denver. I was seven then. He took me to Santa Fe, then to Tucson, where he worked for the Southern Overland Mail."

"Then he started his own line in Yucca Flats."

Alec nodded. He looked out across the darkening slope.

Denny threw away his stick. "I've got a feeling he'll get this road through in time."

"I hope so," said Alec quietly.

A faint light appeared in the east. The new moon was rising over the bulky Grindstones. In an hour, the two boys could see the road far below them. It was colder now, with a keening wind sweeping through the pass.

Denny sat up straight. "Listen," he said.

"I can't hear anything."

Denny stared down at the road. Denny had hearing like a dog. "I heard something, Alec."

Minutes ticked past with agonizing slowness. Then, as though materialized by some supernatural shaman out of moonbeams and shadows, there appeared on the road the figure of a mounted Apache. He rode softly toward the south. His pony must have had on rawhide boots. The Tonto carried a rifle across his naked thighs. His thick hair was banded with a white cloth. He constantly turned his head from side to side as he tested the night with his senses.

Alec froze. Apaches could hear like animals.

The Apache was even with them now. Alec hoped the horses would not whinny or neigh. Sound would carry far in the quiet night. The Tonto rode on and then halted his mount fifty yards down the road. He sat there as if listening. Then he rode onward and vanished out of sight.

"Look!" said Denny hoarsely.

Four more warriors appeared on the road. The wind shifted, and they could be heard talking to one another in their slurring tones. Then, they too, rode below the two boys and disappeared beyond the trees bordering the road.

Alec let his blanket slide from his shoulders. He checked his Sharps and then unhooked his canteen from his belt. Alec placed a hand on Denny's shoulder. "Stay here."

"Where you going?"

"Down there."

"You loco?"

"Sit tight. I won't be long."

Chapter Seven

ALEC WORKED HIS WAY DOWN THE SLOPE, taking advantage of every scrap of cover. His throat was dry, and his heart seemed to pound loudly enough to be heard. Alec crawled through the thick brush in the direction the warriors had gone. He was close to the trees when some sixth sense seemed to warn him to look back. A hundred yards behind him, he could see many mounted warriors on the road. They were sitting their horses, looking to the south.

Alec slid into a gully and wormed his way up the far side. Dust tickled his nostrils, and he had all he could do from exploding into a violent sneeze. He thrust a finger under his nose and concentrated on not sneezing. When the urge had passed, he actually felt weak from the tension.

Alec crouched beneath a bush and looked back down the road. The first five warriors had reappeared and were riding toward their mates. Alec could hear their low voices as the scouts talked and pointed back down the road. One of the warriors touched his horse with his heels and waved on the others. They rode toward a bend in the road and passed beyond a *bosque* of trees.

Alec shifted his position, moving across the gully and up a rough rise until he could see over the trees. For a moment, he saw nothing, and then the warriors appeared. Their leader rode up a talus slope toward a narrow gorge mouth that debouched into the pass. There was an eerie feeling in Alec as he watched them vanish into the gorge, for he could hear no sounds.

Alec waited for a time and then went back to Denny. "Did you see where they went?" he asked.

Denny nodded. "And I was glad to see them go. I don't feel so brave now, Alec."

"Me neither."

"Let's pull foot out of here."

Alec shook his head. "Go back to the horses and keep them quiet."

"What are you going to do?"

"Find out where those bucks went."

Denny gripped Alec's arm. "No, you don't! By Jiminy, Alec, I'll whup you if you try!"

"Listen, Denny: Dance and his men will be coming through here before long. If they don't know those Apaches are in here, they may get ambushed. If I can see where those warriors have gone. I can warn Dance."

Denny's face was pale in the moonlight. "Let me go with you then."

Alec knew it took all the nerve Denny had to make

the offer. He wasn't feeling so courageous himself right now. "No. If anything happens, you high-tail it back down the road and try to find Dance."

Denny stood up and gripped his carbine. "Yeh," he said. "I don't like the idea of you following those bucks, though."

"Neither do I, but it has to be done."

Denny nodded. "My stepfather says a boy grows into a man so fast out in this country he hardly knows it. I guess we're getting pretty close to being men now, ain't we, Alec?"

"I don't feel like a man right now, Denny."

Denny picked up the blankets and walked up the slope. As Alec reached the deserted road, he looked back. He could see Denny watching him. Utter loneliness swept over Alec and he almost started to run back up the slope to be with his companion, but something stronger drove him on — the thought of Dance Birney and his men being trapped in that gorge.

Alec cut quickly across the road and plowed through some shin-tangle brush until he reached the talus slope. There was no sound other than the wind and the faint scraping of branches against each other.

He walked softly into the narrow gorge. It was a foolhardy thing to do, for they might have left guards behind, but Alec had to know whether or not they had gone far beyond the pass.

The moon was full up when he reached the top of the gorge, where he faded into the brush. Alec could see along the top of the heights. Here and there, he could make out warriors stationed among the brush and rocks, where they could watch the road far below them. They were waiting for something and that something must be either Dan Packard's work gang or Dance Birney's party.

Alec looked over the trees to the west. There was a jagged, knife-edged ridge rising at a slant to the north. If riflemen could get up there, unseen and unheard, they could make the lip of the pass untenable for the warriors. There was no sign of any Tontos up on the ridge. They were so sure of their clever ambush!

Alec went back down the gorge, trying not to hurry, although fear seemed to walk close behind him, seeming to breathe foully and icily at the back of his neck. He was reminded of something his father had read to him, part of "The Ancient Mariner."

"...walks on, and turns no more his head, because he knows a frightful fiend Doth close behind him tread."

He crossed the road at a place where he knew he was shielded from the keen eyes high above him.

He was across the road and into the brush when he heard the whinny of a horse. He looked up the slope, mentally castigating Denny for letting a horse make such a noise. Then he realized the noise had come from the south.

Alec crouched behind a rock and cocked his carbine. His hands shook as he checked the cap on the nipple.

Then he saw a tall horseman standing his mount on the road and looking to the north. There was no mistaking Dance Birney. A flood of relief poured through Alec. Alec padded through the brush. "Dance Birney," he called softly.

Dance moved like a frightened lizard. He slid from the saddle, jerking his carbine from its sheath, then slapped his horse on the rump, and vanished into the brush on the far side of the road.

Alec raised his head. "Dance! It's me! Alec King!"

"Show yourself!"

Alec stood up in the moonlight.

Dance stood up. "You little fool!" he snapped. "I've got a good mind to wale you right here!"

Alec crossed the road. Dance's face was drawn and tense. "There is a war party of Tontos about three-quarters of a mile north of here," said Alec quickly.

Dance looked north. "Where's your horse?"

"Denny Morris has our horses."

Dance grounded his Spencer carbine. "So he's here too? Do you two boys realize the trouble you've caused? They're looking all over for you!"

Alec looked down at the ground. "We were only trying to help, Dance," he said quietly.

"Well, there's no use in waling you now. Your pa will take care of that. Get Denny and bring those horses down here."

Alec climbed the slope. He whistled softly. Denny thrust his head up over a boulder. "What's up, scout?" he asked.

Alec pointed down the slope. "Dance Birney is down there."

"Whew! I'll bet he gave you the whatfor."

They led the horses down the slope to the road.

Dance shook his head as he saw them. "As if I didn't have enough troubles," he said coldly. "Come on. The boys are down the road."

A man stood up behind a rock ledge as they reached a bend in the road. He raised his Spencer and then lowered it as he recognized them. "You found the kids," he said.

"Yes, Ory," said Dance. "Where are the others?"

"Down the road about a quarter of a mile."

The four of them walked south along the road until they heard a soft whistle. Ed Schmidt stood up from the brush. His face was taut as he saw the two boys. He raised his right arm and shook a big fist. "Man," he said, "you two boys got a good licking coming to you."

The rest of the men came out of the brush with ready Spencers. Marty Roe, a tall, redheaded man, strode toward Denny. He gripped Denny by the arm. "Your pa said I was to take care of you while he was away," he said. "If anything had happened to you, he would have killed me."

"Let him be," said Dance. "The damage is done."

Marty turned. "He's my nephew, ain't he? I'll do with him what I please."

"I told you to let him be."

Roe released Denny. "You ain't telling me what to do, Birney," he said coldly. "Who do you think you are? General Sherman?"

Dance raised his head. "As long as I'm in charge here, Marty, you'll do as I say or head back for Yucca Flats."

Marty Roe spat. Then he walked away. Dance Birney had a way of handling older men. Alec had seen him do it more than once. There was always a quiet authority in his voice.

Dance leaned against a tree. "Tell them what you saw, Alec."

Alec took out his sheath knife and found a patch of soft earth. The moonlight was almost as bright as the day. "Here's the pass," he said, drawing a deep notch into the ground. "A narrow gorge cuts to the west here." He marked it at an angle to the pass mark. "North of the gorge is where they are, lined along the lip of the pass, where they can watch the road."

"How many of them?" asked Dance.

"Thirty or forty. I'm not quite sure."

"How can we get at them?"

Alec drew a line west of the mark he had made that indicated the pass. "There's a ridge here, running parallel to their position and behind it. It's about fifty yards higher than the place where they are."

Dance rubbed his lean jaw. He looked up at the craggy side of the pass. "If we could work our way up behind them, we could ambush our would-be ambushers."

Bartolome Madera spoke up. "There is a way to get up there. I have hunted often in here. I know the place Alec told us about. It is hard going, though, and we cannot take the horses."

"Can we make it up there before dawn?"

"In the moonlight, it is possible. In the darkness, I am not so sure."

Dance looked at the men. "Are you willing to try?"

Kirby Todd grinned. "I didn't come in here all this way just to turn and run for home because a few Tontos are waiting for us."

"Count me in," said Marty Roe. "I'd like to get a crack at somebody soon." His eyes held Dance's as he spoke.

"I'll go," said quiet George Barren.

The rest of the men nodded. Dance smashed his right fist into his left palm. "Then we'll do it! Dan Packard and his men are some miles behind us. They figured on being here just about dawn. Cass, you ride back and hurry him up. Tell him not to worry but to keep his men ready for action. We'll do the rest. I want him to come through here as if there weren't a Tonto buck for fifty miles."

"Live bait," said Cass with a grin. He led his horse south along the road.

The men led their horses into a branch canyon and picketed them half a mile from the road. Dance held up a hand. "Slim, you will stay here with the horses and the two boys."

Alec walked up to Dance. "I'm going along," he said.

"You think so? I'm in command here, kid."

"I know exactly where they are, Dance."

"He's right," said Slim. "Besides, if the Tontos come back here, I'll have to take off like a jackrabbit. He's safer with you."

"I'll go too," said Denny. His voice broke a little as he spoke.

Dance looked at Marty Roe. Marty shrugged. "The kids will be safer with us, Dance. I'm sorry I riled you."

"Forget it."

Bob Porter spoke up. "I've got a game leg. I doubt if I could make that climb. I'll stay with Slim, Dance, if it's all right with you."

"Good," said Dance.

They took their carbines, water canteens, and magazine boxes and followed Bartolome up the canyon. He began to ascend a steep slope on the northern side of the canyon.

It took them over an hour to gain the heights. They dropped on the ground for a breather. They all were out of breath. Alec rubbed a place where catclaw had ripped open a trouser leg and cut into his thigh. Ben Richmond was busy prying a cactus needle from his boot.

"Come on," said Dance. He followed Bartolome through the thorny brush.

The moon was on the wane when they came up under the western side of the knife-edged ridge. Dance climbed the ridge with Alec. They squatted in the brush at the top and looked down on the pass brim. Alec pointed out the waiting warriors. Dance nodded. "Scared, Alec?" he asked.

Alec nodded.

"So am I. Stick close to me when the shooting starts."

Dance rubbed the breech of his Spencer. "We can

give them chain lightning and eleven claps of thunder with these, Alec."

Alec looked down at the Tontos. Some of them were painting themselves for war.

Dance went down to the men. In a little while, they reached the ridge top, moving like Apaches themselves. The men spread out along the ridge to find good shooting positions. The moon was almost gone. The wind keened across the ridge. A coyote howled far down in the darkened pass. Another one gave voice farther to the south.

"Melancholy beggars those coyotes," said George Barren softly.

"Gives a man the creeps," said Ory Carter.

Bartolome Madera lowered his canteen. "Those are Tontos," he said softly.

The men looked at one another. Hands gripped carbines.

Denny crawled up beside Alec. "I don't know whether I like this or not," he whispered.

"We can't go back now," said Alec.

"That's for sure."

They lay quietly, listening to the soft sounds of the night. Alec closed his eyes. He was playing a man's game now. There was no going back for any of them.

Chapter Eight

"WAKE UP!" SAID THE VOICE CLOSE TO ALEC'S
ear. He started up as a hard hand closed over his
mouth. He looked up into the dim face of Dance
Birney. "It's almost dawn," said the coach driver.

Alec shivered a little in the cold wind. He felt for
his Sharps. Denny Morris was crouched behind a
boulder, with his carbine resting atop it. He grinned
weakly at Alec. Alec crawled over beside his friend.
Denny opened his mouth and then closed it. Alec
checked his Sharps as Denny checked his weapon.

"Suppose they rush us?" asked Denny.

Alec looked at him. "We shoot."

"Yeh, but if they get among us. We ain't got
repeaters."

Alec nodded. "It's too late to trade in our Sharps,"
he said. He took out his Colt and twirled the cylinder.
He placed the little five-shooter between them.

"My pa said always to leave one last cartridge in
case you're going to be captured," said Denny.

"Talk about something else, will you?"

"What, for instance?"

"I wish I knew."

The men were stirring all along the ridge. Dance crawled along the line, speaking softly to each man.

The false dawn began to lighten the eastern sky. Objects heretofore shrouded in darkness began to stand out.

Quietly, the men began to check their repeaters. Magazine boxes were opened for easy access to the magazine tubes. Rear sights were flipped up and adjusted for the range.

"How far do you make it?" asked Denny of Alec, jerking a thumb down toward the position of the Tontos.

"About one hundred and fifty yards."

"More likely one hundred and seventy-five."

Bartolome Madera grinned. "You sound like a couple of sharpshooters," he said.

"We are," said Alec, but there was no conviction in his voice. He had shot at targets up to a hundred yards and had once dropped an antelope at one hundred and fifty yards, but he had always considered that a lucky shot. Besides, it was one thing to shoot at a target or an antelope and quite another to shoot at a maddened Tonto buck who was shooting back at you.

Alec flipped up his rear sight and raised the slide to about one hundred and fifty yards. He wished he had a long-barreled Sharps rifle now rather than the shorter and less accurate carbine.

The light began to grow, and then there was a faint

flush of sunlight showing just beyond the eastern heights. A bird called sleepily from the brush.

Alec stared down the rough slope until his eyes hurt, trying to spot a Tonto, but it seemed as if they had vanished.

"You see any of 'em?" asked Denny hoarsely.

"No."

"Maybe they've pulled foot," said Denny hopefully.

"They're there," said George Barren.

"How do you know?" asked Denny.

George shrugged. "I can *feci* them," he said.

The ridge top was quiet as the sun tipped the eastern mountains. The pass was still deep in shadows. The wind shifted, blowing up toward them now.

Fletch Proctor hunched his jacket collar higher on his neck. "Reminds me of the war," he said. "We was waiting in the woods at Cold Harbor just like this. Couldn't see a reb anywheres. Then the command comes to charge. I jumps over the breastworks and crashes through the brush. When I reaches the rebel breastworks, I looks behind me. I was all alone. The Minie balls was humming like bees past me. I thinks maybe I'm the only man in the whole Fifth Corps out there."

"So?" asked Bartolome.

Fletch shifted his chew of tobacco and spat leisurely. "I looks up and sees a cannon staring me right in the eye. The gunner jerks the lanyard. The cannon goes off in my face."

Denny Morris stared at him. "What happened then, Fletch?"

Fletch Proctor yawned. "Why, Sonny, I was kilt dead right there on the spot."

Denny flushed as the nearby men laughed softly.

"That's an old chestnut," said George Barren.

Dance Birney crawled along the line. "Shut up," he said tensely. "You sound like a bunch of jays chattering in the pinons."

Alec felt better for the laugh. Fletch Proctor could tell a better story than any man in Yucca Flats.

An Apache stood up from his hiding place. He looked down the pass. Two more Apaches stood up. One of them wore a mat of yellow fur on his head from which protruded two yellow-stained horns. Parallel streaks of white-clay paint showed across his beak of a nose and his cheekbones. He looked like a demon conjured straight from Hades. He padded along the line, arousing his warriors. They began to show themselves. Some of them began to touch up their paint.

The warrior with the horned headdress wore a deerskin shirt which flapped about his thighs. "Medicine shirt," said George Barren softly. "They think they are invulnerable when they wear them."

Bartolome Madera rested his Spencer on a rock and sighted it at the chief. "That is Diabolito, I'm sure," he said. "I will soon show him how invulnerable that shirt is."

"Don't shoot!" snapped Dance.

Bartolome smiled. "I won't. But he is mine. I know him. He raided my uncle's *estancia* near Turret Peak and slaughtered my uncle and his whole family. He is a great warrior and a great thief, but Bartolome Madera will soon end his life. This, I promise."

Alec looked at the set face of the Mexican. Bartolome was usually always smiling. He always led the first dance at the Mexican *bailes* held in Yucca Flats and had composed many gay *versos* for the songs sung by his people, but now he had changed, and the change boded no good for Diabolito — The Little Devil.

The Apaches were checking their weapons. Dance took out a pair of field glasses and focused them on the Tontos. He lowered the glasses. "Repeaters," he said. "Henry rifles. They look as if they're fresh out of the factory grease. They have full bandoleers of cartridges, too."

"Where do you suppose they get them?" asked Fletch.

"*¿Quién sabe?* Who knows? But I do know this: they had all types of beat-up single-shots not more than a few months ago. Someone is running guns into them."

"Look!" said Kirby Todd. "They've heard something!"

The Apaches were looking down the pass. It was getting lighter down there. Then the wind shifted, and the men on the ridge could hear the faint rumbling of wheels, the thudding of many hoofs, and the popping of whips.

"Dan Packard," said Dance. "Right on schedule."

The Tontos sank down into cover. In a few minutes, the brim of the pass looked deserted.

Spencer levers were operated, pushing cartridges into chambers. The men shifted and moved their carbines into better positions.

"Pick your man and shoot at him until he goes down," said Dance to George Rarren. "Pass the word along."

The command was passed on down the line.

"No shooting until I give the word," said Dance.

Dance's last order was passed from man to man.

Alec full-cocked his Sharps but kept his finger away from the trigger. One shot would alert the Tontos, and they would be gone like a gaggle of frightened geese.

Then suddenly, a lone horseman passed along the road. It was Cass Willis. The man rode as though he were on the main street of Yucca Flats. It took nerve not to look up at the heights to the west of the pass road.

Dan Packard appeared just ahead of his lead wagon. The driver handled his reins with a long-barreled rifle resting across his thighs. Then, one after the other, a line of wagons appeared, heavily laden and groaning as they took the ascent. Whips popped steadily. The big draft horses strained against their collars. There were now ten wagons in the pass, followed by several riders with rifles across their thighs.

Diabolito moved. He raised his repeater and sighted it. His warriors followed his example.

Dance stood up and sighted his carbine. "Now!" he yelled. His voice echoed from the heights and was instantly drowned out by the crash of carbines. Smoke swirled back on the men. Alec had fired, then pushed forward the breech lever. He fumbled a linen-covered cartridge into the breech and raised the breech lever. The sharp forward edge of the breechblock sheared off the end of the cartridge. He placed a cap on the nipple and full-cocked the stubby carbine. Then, and only then, did he look down at the Tontos.

The men were churning out bullets from their Spencers. The Tontos were scattering under the deadly fire. Down on the road, the wagoners had dropped on the far sides of their wagons and were firing up at the brim of the canyon.

Smoke drifted off before the wind, and the shattering echoes of the roaring Spencers echoed and re-echoed throughout the narrow pass.

"Pour it to 'em!" cried out Dance. His command was superfluous, as the men were firing as fast as they could load and pull trigger.

Denny Morris yelled. "I think I winged one!"

"Braggart," said Alec. He fired at a running buck and was sure he saw the Tonto stagger in his stride. Some of the Tontos were plunging down the slope like great, ungainly birds to avoid the deadly fire from behind them. Slugs ripped into them from the embattled wagoners. They kept up a steady fire from the shelter of the wagons.

The Tontos turned north and darted into the cover of rocks and trees, throwing frantic shots behind them as they stampeded from that place of death. In a few minutes, those who had not fallen were out of sight.

"Cease fire!" roared Dance.

A few scattered shots rang out, and then came the metallic patter of ejected brass shell cases on the rocky ground.

"Reload!" commanded Dance.

Butt gates were pushed open, and tin tubes of cartridges were placed at the openings. The Spencers were quickly reloaded.

"Stay where you are!" yelled Dance.

The smoke drifted up the canyon, raveled by the wind. Here and there, among the rocks and brush, lay the bodies of the Tontos who had been felled by the leaden storm.

Bartolome Madera raised a fist. "I missed him," he said.

Fletch Proctor grinned. "Maybe that battle shirt of his saved him, *ami go.*"

"I'll get him someday."

Alec felt as though his throat had been scrubbed with ashes. He felt for his canteen and filled his mouth with the cold water. Denny Morris reached for the canteen. "Me too," he said.

"Scared?" asked George Barren.

"Yen," said Denny. "Weren't you, George?"

The quiet man nodded. "I'll never get used to killing," he said.

Dance Birney shoved back his hat. "I know," he said quietly, "but they would have wiped out Packard and his men if we hadn't done some killing. Poor devils. Someone is giving them those new rifles and stirring them up."

"Such as?" asked Ory Carter.

"I don't know, but I aim to find out."

Dance slid down the forward slope of the ridge. His carbine was cocked and ready.

"Be careful," said Bartolome to Alec and Denny.

"The wounded ones are dangerous. Watch for them. They will play possum, and all of a sudden, there is a knife in your belly."

Denny paled. He quickly reloaded his carbine.

The men worked their way down the slope. Alec walked south and passed around the scene of the fighting. He had no stomach to see what they had done. Denny trotted along behind him.

They reached the road and then heard a hoarse scream followed by a quick shot. Smoke rose from the heights.

Dan Packard walked over to Alec and Denny. He was a big man dressed in sober, dusty black. He held a Henry rifle in his hands. "You boys all right?" he asked. "Your father was worried sick about you, Alec."

Dance came through the brush. "He's all right, Dan. Did a man's work for us. He located the Tontos and told us where they were."

"Denny helped me," said Alec. He felt a little queasy.

"What happened up there?" asked Denny.

Dance looked up the slope. Two men were supporting Ben Richmond. Blood stained his right trouser leg. "Ben walked right into a wounded buck. He got at Ben with his knife, but Bartolome killed him."

"How many of them did you get, Dance?" asked Dan.

"Nine," said Dance quietly. "A dirty business."

"You saved the wagons and my men," said Dan.

Dance waved a hand.

The men came down from the heights. Ory Carter and Bartolome walked north along the road, with ready carbines, to scout theContos.

Dan wiped the sweat from his broad face. "I think they'll let us alone for a time now," he said. "They got a terrible lesson, Dance."

One of the wagoners led off a badly wounded horse.

A shot rang out from beside the road. The wagoner appeared with a smoking pistol in his hand. "Poor Jim," he said quietly. "I hated to do that. He was my best hoss."

Dan grounded his carbine. "I'll leave you four men, Dan."

"Thanks. I'll work my men close together and have them keep their rifles handy. I'll keep guards out at night."

"How soon can you get started on the road?"

"As soon as my men get some breakfast."

Fires were started beside the road. The aroma of coffee and frying bacon mingled with the redolent odors of the brush now being warmed by the sun.

Alec and Denny ate with Dance and Dan. Alec didn't have much appetite.

Dan looked kindly at Alec. "I know how you feel," he said.

Alec looked away. Denny took bacon from a spider that sizzled over a fire. He placed the thick strips on bread and formed a huge sandwich. He looked at it and then at Alec. Then he put the sandwich down. "Suddenly, I don't feel hungry, Alec," he said miserably.

The rest of the men were wolfing down thick bacon sandwiches. Even lien Richmond, with his bandaged leg, was doing full justice to the food. *How do they do it?* wondered Alec.

As if he had read Alec's thoughts, Dan Packard spoke up. "Remember that these men are mostly war veterans and Indian fighters, Alec," said the engineer. "War is a business for them. In time, you may get hardened to this type of thing."

"I hope not," said Alec.

The men who were to go back to Yucca Flats, walked down the sunlit road to their horses. Alec looked back toward the heights as he walked between Dance and Denny. Somewhere back there, he had lost some of his boyhood, and he knew it would never come back again.

Chapter Nine

THEY REACHED YUCCA FLATS LATE IN THE afternoon of the next day, and the men dispersed to their homes. Denny Morris had learned that his father and mother had not yet returned to Yucca Flats, so he accompanied Dance and Alec to the King Line office. The office was empty, but in a little while, Bert King came in. He looked at Alec. "How are you, Son?" he asked.

Alec had expected a verbal lashing from his father. "All right," he said.

His father sat down at his desk. "I should reprimand you," he said, "but Ed Schmidt told me of the fine work you did. I'll forgive you this time, but Alec, don't ever leave here without permission again."

"I won't," promised Alec.

"That goes for you too, Denny," said Bert King.

Denny flushed. "I couldn't let Alec go alone," he said.

Dance laughed. Bert King smiled. "All right. You're a good *compañero*, Denny. Alec is lucky to have a friend like you."

Denny grinned. "It goes both ways, Mr. King."

Dance eyed Bert King keenly. "What's wrong, Bert? You should be as happy as a bear in a honey tree right now, what with the Tonto menace taken care of and the road being worked on again."

Alec's father nodded. "I am, in that respect, but I've had more trouble."

"Such as?"

"The day after you left, Charley Lee was driving the northbound stagecoach through Owl Pass. He was ambushed at just about the same place Mike Tagger got it. A slug right through his chest. Three bags of mail were taken along with some express packages. It was done by Apaches."

"How is Charley?"

Bert looked away. "He died at Caballo swing station."

Dance shook his head. "You're sure it was Apaches?"

"Lije Parsons said he was sure they did it."

"But he didn't see them?"

"No."

"Did Charley talk before he died?"

"No. He was in a coma."

"Any passengers?"

"None."

Dance whistled softly. "Owl Pass," he said. "I can't

understand it. They avoid that place like they would a cemetery."

"The fact is that Charley was murdered, and the mail and express packages are missing."

Bert King got up and paced back and forth. "We haven't had a passenger since that happened. You know I run my coaches without guards to cut down expenses. Now, Ross Corson has assigned two well-armed guards for each of his coaches. He's getting all the passenger trade."

"That figures."

"I can assign guards, but I'm shorthanded as it is. I'll have to cut down the number of runs and place guards on the few coaches I can get through."

Bert King looked at his wall map. He idly took something from his vest pocket and flipped it up and down in his big hands. It fell to the floor. Dance picked it up and held it up to the light. It was a mutilated bullet. "What's this, Bert?" he asked.

Bert turned. "That? It was taken from Charley's body. It's the slug that killed him."

Dance studied it. "About fifty caliber, isn't it?"

"It's a fifty-four."

Dance took out the brass cartridge case Alec had found in Owl Pass the evening he had brought Mike Tagger out. Dance fitted the base of the bullet into the brass case. It was a perfect fit. He looked at Alec. "Burnside?" he said.

Alec nodded. "Sure looks like it."

"What does that mean?" asked his father.

"Alec picked this up where Mike was ambushed. Ed Schmidt identified it as a Burnside cartridge."

Bert scratched his jaw. "Doesn't mean much. I've seen many Burnside carbines in my time out here."

Dance threw the slug up and down in his big hand. "I still think it's outright peculiar about Apaches' being in Owl Pass."

Bert looked quickly at him. "You don't suppose the job was done by road agents, do you?"

"I'm not supposing anything. But I still say Apaches won't go near Owl Pass."

They looked at each other. "There haven't been any road agents in this area for a long time," said Bert.

Dance walked to the window and looked across the street at the Corson Line office. "Maybe somebody is sending them out—the same man perhaps who is supplying repeating rifles to the Tontos."

"Ross Corson?"

"¿Quién sabe? Who would gain the most by driving you out of business?"

"It's fantastic!"

"Maybe. But I'm going to find out if any of Corson's men carry a Burnside carbine."

"Be careful, Dance."

Dance grinned. "I always am."

"Alec," said his father, "you go on home and get cleaned up. Take Denny with you. He's going to stay with us until his father and mother get home. That way, I can keep an eye on both of you."

"Suits me," said Denny cheerfully, "because I haven't had so much fun in a long time."

"Fun," said Dance. "I'll fun *you*, Denny!"

The two boys walked up the street. Denny looked back over his shoulder. " I wonder if Ross Corson is really trying to put your father out of business, Alec?"

"I wouldn't put it past him."

"Me neither."

Alec gripped Denny by the shoulder. "Maybe we can do a little nosing around by ourselves and find out."

"Remember what your father said," warned Denny.

"We won't leave town. He didn't say anything about our staying around Yucca Flats and doing nothing, did he?"

"Nope. I'm with you all the way, *amigo*."

———

AFTER DINNER, Bert King filled his pipe and lighted it, and began to study his ledgers. Someone knocked on the door. Alec opened it. A tall man stood on the porch. "Hello, Alec," he said. "Is your father at home?"

"Hello. Mr. Horton. Yes, he's in."

Alec ushered the man into the living room. "Hello, Fred," said Alec's father. He held out his hand. "I think I know what brings you here."

"Who's he?" whispered Denny to Alec.

"Fred Horton, the postal inspector."

The two boys walked into the kitchen. They could see the two men through the open door.

Fred Horton sat down. "That was a nasty business in Owl Pass, Bert," he said quietly.

"Yes."

"Too bad about Charley."

Bert King nodded. "He was a good man and a top driver."

"You've found no traces of the mail?"

"None."

Horton lighted a cigar and watched the smoke rise. "How's the new road coming along?"

"Dan Packard is back at work out there."

"Will he have it done in time for you to keep your schedule into Tres Cabezas?"

"I hope so."

"I have instructions to turn the franchise over to Ross Corson if you don't. I don't like to do it, but I have my orders. Corson has influential friends who will see that he gets it."

"I wish I had a few influential friends."

Horton leaned forward. "I have two men looking about Owl Pass for traces of the mail and express packages. Have you learned anything about the holdup?"

"Nothing."

"It puts me in a bad spot. My superiors have been after me ever since Mike Tagger was held up in the pass. They say if you can't safeguard the mail, they'll have to pull your franchise."

Bert King relighted his pipe. "More of Corson's work?"

"He had nothing to do with it. We're concerned

with getting the mail through, not with rivalries between competing stage companies."

"I'm sorry, Fred. I'm on edge."

"I understand. Can you give me any good news on the new run to Tres Cabezas?"

"Dan is working, as I said. I'll have my stations equipped and manned as soon as I can."

"I heard there was trouble with the Tontos in there."

"Yes. But Dance Birney and some of the boys gave them a lesson."

"Too bad the army can't help you. I'll see what I can do."

"It's no use. I wrote to Major Johnson at Fort Irland. He's got his hands full with marauding Apaches south of here. He said he'd try to get me some guards in the next month or so."

"But too late to help, eh?"

Bert King nodded.

Fred Horton stood up. "You've still got a little time. I hope you can make the grade, Bert. If not, the mail franchise will be turned over to Ross Corson. You understand that it will be none of my doing. I've got my job to do."

"It's all right, Fred. Thanks, anyway."

When Horton had left, Bert King shoved back his ledgers and rested his head on his arms.

Alec softly closed the door. "Come on, Denny," he said.

"Whereto?"

"To bed, you dummy!"

They washed and then went to bed. Moonlight shone through the window. Denny locked his hands behind his red head. "I wish we could help your pa," he said.

"We will."

"How?"

Alec leaned close to his friend. "When Dad goes to bed you and I will sneak out of the house and take a little stroll."

"Where?"

"To the Beacon." My stepfather would wale the tar outa me if he knew I was in there. He don't cotton to drinking or smoking."

Alec grinned. "We're not going *in* there, Denny. Ross Corson's men hang out in there. They leave their horses at the hitching rail. If they have rifles or carbines, they'll be left hanging to their saddles."

"So?"

"We're going to look for a Burnside carbine on those horses."

There was a soft step in the hall. Both boys closed their eyes. The door opened quietly. Alec peeked out of one eye. His father came in and looked down at them. "Asleep, Son?" he asked.

"Just about."

His father pulled the comforter higher on them. "You've had quite an adventure, Son," he said.

"What happens if we lose the line, Dad?"

His father shrugged. "I can always get a job as a station manager on the Southern Overland."

"Away from Yucca Flats?"

"Yes. We'll have to start anew. Alec. Good night."

The door closed behind Bert King. Alec sat up. Denny shook his head. "You won't lose the line, Aiec," he said stoutly. "I'll see to that!"

Chapter Ten

THE BOYS WAITED FOR HALF AN HOUR BEFORE they slipped out of bed and dressed quickly. They left the room by the window and padded softly around the darkened house until they reached the street and then they took off down the empty street toward the center of town.

The Beacon hitching rail was lined with horses of all colors and sizes. "Stay by the window, Denny," whispered Alec. "Whistle twice if anyone comes out of the Beacon."

Denny got up on the sidewalk and stationed himself by the large front window of the establishment.

Alec started down the line of horses, drawing carbines and rifles out of their leather scabbards in order to identify them. Halfway down the line, he had found only Winchesters, a Spencer or two and one issue single-shot Springfield carbine. A horse nickered loudly in the quiet as Alec approached him. Alec stroked the bay's nose and talked softly to him until he quieted down and allowed Alec to examine the carbine that was strapped to his saddle. It was another Winchester.

Denny whistled twice. Alec faded into the shadows. A man pushed through the batwing doors of the Beacon, stamped onto the boardwalk with a loud jingling of spurs, and then untethered a big claybank. He swung up into his saddle and paused to roll a cigarette. The light of the match revealed his face. He was a total stranger. Alec had not yet checked the man's saddle gun.

The man glanced at him. "Ain't you up kinda late, Sonny?"

"I'm looking for my dog," lied Alec.

"What kind of dog?"

"A mutt. Yellowish color with a black face."

The man laughed. "Colorful, ain't he?"

Alec stopped by the horse. "Your girth is loose," he said.

"So? Thanks."

The man dismounted to check his girth. Alec walked around the horse and drew the man's gun from its sheath. The man came up behind him. "What are you doing? My girth is tight enough."

A big hand clamped on Alec's neck. "You trying to steal my Henry rifle?"

Alec shook his head. "I just like to look at guns."

"Well, look at somebody else's gun then." The man shoved Alec toward the saloon porch and then mounted. "Smart kid," he said as he kneed his horse out into the center of the street.

Alec quickly checked all the rest of the saddle guns. There wasn't a Burnside in the lot. "Come on, Denny," he said.

Denny trotted to Alec. "No luck?"

"None."

"Funny thing. Ross Corson is usually in the Beacon every night with Rig Conboy. Ain't neither one of them in there tonight. What do we do now?"

"We'll check the horses at the Miner's Rest and at the Union House."

"We're really doing the town tonight."

In an hour, the two boys were trudging back up the street from the Union House, which was at the far southern end of the town beside a branch creek that met Yucca Creek. Not one saddle gun had been a Burnside.

"I guess my idea wasn't so good," said Alec wearily.

"Either the man who shot Charley Lee isn't in town or he keeps his Burnside hidden somewhere else."

"What time is it?"

"Close to midnight."

The moon was low over the hills to the west of town. Alec yawned. "We'd better get some sleep," said Alec.

Denny stopped suddenly. "Lookit that light down there!"

There was a flickering light showing against the

drab frame buildings farther along the main street. Alec began to run. "A fire!" he yelled. "Ring the bell, Denny! It's our wagon shed!"

Alec slammed his feet hard against the rutted street. Denny darted toward the big bell that hung in a gallows framework near the jailhouse.

A tongue of flame licked hungrily along the side of the big door at the side of the shed. The light of the flames showed through the dirty windows.

The big bell began to clang, echoing from the low hills. Lights flared up in houses along the street, and then doors began to bang open. A man yelled. "It's the King Line wagon shed!"

A man cut across the street in front of Alec. "Turn out the fire volunteers!" he cried. Alec ran headlong into the man and knocked him sprawling. He hurdled the fallen man and reached the big shed. Flames crackled hungrily at the sun-dried wood. Horses began to neigh in shrill fright from the stables next to the shed.

Alec jerked open the front door of the shed. A wave of hot smoke gushed out at him. He staggered back, gasping for breath. The bell was clanging steadily, arousing the whole town. Men dashed out of the saloons and ran for the firehouse. The doors were opened, and half-dressed men hauled the pumper cart from the firehouse and grabbed hold of the draglines.

Alec peered into the shed. Flames were licking up the varnished sides of the Concords. One of them sagged suddenly as a burned thoroughbrace gave way.

The coach fell sideways, and fire gushed from its interior.

The pumper cart slid to a halt across the street, and the end of the hose was thrust into a water reservoir. Men gripped the handles and began to pump as the hose-men ran across the street toward the burning shed. A spurt of water splashed against the smoking wood.

The horses were thrashing in their stalls. Alec ran to the stables and opened the door. Smoke drifted throughout the interior. Alec jerked off his jacket and pulled open a stall door. A big chestnut in the stall whinnied shrilly. Alec threw his coat over the horse's eyes and led him from the stable.

"The kid has the right idea!" cried out Joe Simmons, the liveryman.

A powerful wheelhorse kicked out and smashed the wall behind him. Flame shot through the opening. Men ran in and blindfolded the horses to lead them to safety. The last horse had been led out when the rear wall of the stable spurted flames. In minutes, runnels of fire raced along the wall. Hay and straw fed the raging flames. There was a loud crackling sound from the hayloft. A pall of smoke hung over the street.

Alec turned as he heard his father's voice. Bert King stared unbelievingly at the holocaust. As he looked, the roof of the wagon shed collapsed with a roaring noise, and fire shot up fifty feet high. The men at the pumper dragged their hose across the street and began to wet down the false-fronted frame buildings as fat sparks made a Fourth of July display in the street. There was no sense in spraying water on the collapsed wagon shed and the doomed stable.

"How did it start?" asked Ed Schmidt.

"I saw the flames from down the street," said Alec.

Ed shook his head. "The King Line workshops are safe enough as long as the wind is blowing the way it is."

Employees of the King Line company were dousing the roof and walls of the shops. The wind shifted a little, forcing the leaping flames away from them.

Denny Morris came up to Alec. "We were too late," he said.

"Where was the watchman?" asked Bert King.

Ed raised his head. "Jonas Miller was on duty tonight," said he.

"Where is he?"

"I didn't see him around," said Alec.

Bert gripped Ed by the arm. "Find him," he said thinly.

The fire had full control of the stables now. A puff of hot air blew from the loft. Smoke billowed out across the street. Alec walked to the shops. Men were up on the roof stamping out sparks. It seemed as if the whole town was watching the fire. Alec looked at the people. There were two familiar faces missing: Ross Corson and Rig Conboy. Then Alec remembered that Denny had said he hadn't seen them in the Beacon. Hardly a night went by that the precious pair were anywhere else but in the Beacon unless they were out of town.

Ed Schmidt walked toward Bert King, gripping

Jonas Miller by the arm." I found him in the Beacon," he said.

Jonas Miller was a gangling ne'er-do-well who did odd jobs around Yucca Flats. He hiccuped as he saw Bert. Alec's father looked at the drunken watchman. "You were not at your post, Jonas?"

"I only went to get a drink to keep warm," said Miller.

"How long were you gone?"

"Ten minutes, no more."

"He's a liar," said Tom Castle, the shoemaker. "I went in there at ten o'clock, and he was in there then. I left there half an hour ago, and he was still there."

Ed Schmidt cocked a big fist. Alec's father shook his head. "Let him go," he said. "The damage is done."

Ed shoved the watchman. Jonas ran, weaving down the street.

The stable roof collapsed, sending sparks flying through the smoky air. Bert King turned away. He walked slowly to his office and went in. Dance Birney came through the crowd. "Come on, Alec," he said.

Joe Simmons looked at Dance. "The boys can corral your horses behind my livery stable," he said.

"Thanks, Joe," said Dance.

Denny Morris was hard at work helping to work one of the pumper handles. Alec walked with Dance to the office. His father sat at his desk. He shook his head. "That does it, Dance. We've lost every vehicle except three. One of them in Yavapai Wells and two of them awaiting repairs at Caballo swing station. The King Line is through."

Dance rubbed his lean jaw. "There's a fairly good Concord for sale by the Southern Overland in Yavapai Wells. Cheap at twice the price."

Bert King placed his elbows on the desk and rested his head on his hands. "I'll have to have feed for the horses," he said. "I've just enough money to meet this month's payroll."

Dance pulled down his hat. "Wait here," he said. He hurried out into the street.

Alec sat down and looked at his father. He had never seen him so dejected before. His father looked up. "It looks as if we'll be moving on," he said. "I can sell the horses and the house for enough money to keep us for a time until I can get a decent job."

The big clock on the wall ticked steadily on. The excited voices of the firefighters could be heard.

Dance opened the door. "You've got some loyal employees, Bert," he said. "I talked to as many of them as I could find. Every one of them said to skip this month's payroll and make it up when you can."

There was a suspicion of tears in Bert King's gray eyes. "Thanks, Dance."

"I'll need that payroll money, or at least part of it, to get that Concord at Yavapai Wells."

Alec's father nodded. He got up and went into the back room. "Dance!" he called out.

Dance and Alec ran into the little back room. The back door gaped open. Bert was standing near the heavy safe. The door hung open. There was a stench of burnt powder in the close air. Papers from the safe littered the floor. Alec's father turned slowly. "The safe has been blown open. The money is gone!"

Dance Birney darted to the door. He stepped outside and looked up and down the dark alley.

"It's no use," said Bert King. "They're long gone."

Dance came back into the room. He sniffed the air. "They must have blown the safe during all the noise out in the street."

Alec's father kicked shut the safe door. "Well, that's that."

Dance shook his head. "I'll round up enough money for the coach," he said. "Joe Simmons will give you credit for feed."

"You just won't quit, will you, Dance?"

"I've never been licked yet, and I don't intend to start."

"Go ahead then."

They closed the office and walked up the street toward the King house. Behind them were two huge beds of fire, where the collapsed wagon shed and stables still burned.

Denny Morris trotted up behind them, but he was wise enough not to talk.

Dance placed a hand on Alec's shoulder. "I'll take you with me. Alec," he said. "We'll leave in the morning."

"I'd better not leave Dad."

His father looked at him. "Go ahead, Son. You can't do any good here. You'll be of more help to Dance."

Chapter Eleven

YAVAPAI WELLS SWELTERED UNDER THE LATE afternoon sun. A hot, dry wind blew dust and papers along the main street. Dance and Alec tethered their horses to the hitching rail in front of the Western House and walked over to the shops of the Southern Overland. An employee showed them the Concord that was for sale. They inspected the vehicle from top to bottom.

Dance crawled from underneath the coach. He dusted his hands. "It's not in bad shape," said Dance.

Matt Sutliff, the shop manager, came out to them. "What do you think of it, Dance?" he asked.

"It'll do! What's the price?"

"Eight hundred."

"I'll give you seven hundred."

Matt shook his head. "If it was mine, I'd sell it to you for that price. Dance, but the company wants eight hundred."

Dance rubbed his jaw. "I've only got seven hundred," he said.

Matt looked up at the sky. "You think Bert will get his new division through in time to hold his franchise?"

"The whole company is behind him. We're doing our best to get it through."

Matt tugged at his dragoon mustache. "Bert King has done me a lot of favors. I'd like to see him get this coach if he needs it badly enough."

"We had a fire the night before last. The wagon shed and the stables burned to the ground. Every coach was lost, with the exception of three that were out on the division."

Matt shook his head. "Bert's luck has been bad. Tell you what I'll do, Dance. You take the coach. I'll take the seven hundred dollars. I'll pay for the balance, and when Bert can pay me back, the deal will be closed."

Dance grinned. "I had an idea you'd make the deal, Matt."

Matt flushed. "Forget it. Have you got a team to haul the coach into Yucca Flats?"

"The company keeps a reserve team here."

"¡*Bueno!*" Matt slapped Alec on the back. "Tell your father I wish him the best of luck."

"Thanks, Mr. Sutliff."

"Now, I'd like you two to come home with me and have supper with me and the missis."

Dance shook his head. "We're leaving for Caballo station as soon as we can."

"You'll drive at night?"

"Yes. The quicker we get back to Yucca Flats, the better it will be. There's a great deal of work to be done before we open up the new division."

Alec and Dance went to get the reserve team. They led the team to the coach and hitched it up. Alec got the two saddle horses and tethered them behind the coach. They took the coach to Metzger and Company's warehouse to pick up some supplies for the King Line. It was dusk when they drove out onto the road and headed north.

The moon was up when they began the long ascent of Two-Mile Grade. The desert had cooled quickly as soon as the sun had gone down. The coach rocked and swayed as it was pulled up the steep slope. Alec shivered a little. He reached down under the seat and pulled out his jacket. He shrugged into it and turned up the collar.

Dance glanced at Alec. "Seems like we made a good buy," he said.

Alec nodded. "One thing puzzles me though, Dance. Where did you get the seven hundred dollars?"

Dance spoke sharply to the team. "Oh...around."

"Around where?"

Dance grinned. "Just around...that's all."

"I happen to know you spent most of your money on those Spencers."

"That so?"

"That's so!"

Dance snapped his whip over a lagging leader. "I'll

admit my funds were low, but some of the boys at the company came through. But don't tell your dad!"

"I won't. Dance...do the men of the company really think the Tres Cabezas Division will open in time to keep the franchise?"

"Certainly."

Alec shoved his hands deep into his jacket pockets to warm them. He looked at the moonlit ribbon of road ahead of the team and coach. It was almost as though Dance and he had been transported to the moon. There was no sign of life anywhere else. Tall saguaros raised their gaunt arms to the moonlit sky. The yellow sands seemed almost white in the clear rays of the moon.

Dance touched the brake a little. "You see, Alec," he said. "I always believe things will come out right. My mother once told me there is nothing to fear but fear itself. Every time I get afraid, I think of her words. It always works, and things never seem to turn out as badly as you expect them to."

They topped the long grade, and Dance eased the team. The first defile of Owl Pass showed ahead of them. The team trotted along with a jingling of trace chains and a steady drumming of twenty-four hoofs. Then they were in the defile, which rose sharply on each side of them. It was shadowy in the defile, and a cool wind blew toward the Concord. Alec reached down for his Sharps and half-cocked it, placing a cap on the nipple.

"Nervous?" asked Dance.

"Aren't you?"

"Sure. Sure."

The young driver seemed as steady as Gibraltar as he handled the ribbons. But his eyes never stopped scanning the sides of the defile. Alec wished he would open out the team and race through that ominous place at full speed, but Dance drove at a steady mile-eating pace, never varying it a bit.

Alec crawled back over the top of the coach and looked down at the two horses. Biscuits whinnied. Their reins were still tightly tied to the rear of the coach. Alec crawled back and dropped into his seat. "They're okay," he said.

"Getting ready for anything, aren't you?"

Alec nodded. "Foresight is better than hindsight."

They were full into the pass now. The team streamed around the curves, rising higher and higher to reach the crest of the pass road. Alec eyed each bush and boulder, half expecting to see a painted face staring at him over the sights of a rifle.

They were within two hundred yards of the end of the pass, and it was as quiet as a churchyard.

"I guess I was wrong," said Alec.

The splitting noise of a shot echoed his words. Dance jerked a little. He stood up in the boot and lashed out with his whip as another shot crashed out. Alec crawled on top of the coach and hooked his boot toes under the side rails. He saw smoke drifting along the right-hand side of the pass. As he raised his carbine he saw a spurt of orange-red flame and then heard the report of the gun. He sighted and fired at the place where he had seen the flash. He reloaded swiftly. The coach rocked and pitched, and he nearly lost his Sharps over the side.

A gun cracked flatly. The slug rapped into the woodwork of the Concord.

"Hi yup! Hi! Hi! Hi yup! G'lang there!" yelled Dance to the team, punctuating each word with a snap of his long whip.

A fleck of foam from one of the horses' mouths touched Alec's face like a damp kiss. There was no use in trying to shoot accurately, but Alec fired at the last place he had seen a flash and then devoted himself to hanging onto the side rails as the pitching Concord rocketed down the slope, slewed around a curve with a sharp grating of wheels on gravel, and then straightened out to shoot out into the clear.

Alec shook his head. He had nearly gone over the side.

Dance looked back. "The war is over," he said with a grin.

Alec dropped into his seat and reloaded his carbine.

"You want to go back and take a look-see?" asked Dance.

Alec shoved back his hat. "You go if you want to. I'm going on to Caballo."

Dance laughed. He passed the reins to Alec and then slid under him as Alec took the driver's seat. Dance took off his big white hat and poked a finger through a hole in it. "Parted my locks," he said.

Alec felt a little sick as he saw the hole. An inch farther down and Dance would have been killed, and the coach would have probably gone over with him on top of it. He would have been catapulted to the hard ground like a stone from a sling—fair prey for the Apaches.

"Did you see any of them?" asked Dance.

"No."

"How many were there?"

"Not more than one or two."

Dance looked back at the brooding pass. "Odd. Apaches usually don't attack unless they have the advantage."

"Do you think they were Apaches?"

"In there? I've told you before an Apache in his right mind wouldn't go in there."

Alec drove the team to Caballo swing station. The yellow light of the lamp held by Lije Parsons was a welcome sight.

"You loco, Dance?" yelled Lije. "Coming through at night?"

"More romantic, Lije," said Dance cheerily.

"Roll in that Concord," said Lije, pointing over his shoulder to the open gate.

Dance shook his head. "Get us a fresh team, Lije. We're going on tonight."

Lije threw up his free hand in disgust. "Might as well talk to a bull," he said.

Dance climbed up on top of the coach as the team was unharnessed and led away. Alec walked into the quadrangle to say hello to his friends. When he came back, the fresh team was in harness, and Dance was leaning against the side of the gateway, tossing something up and down in his hand. He tossed it to Alec. Alec deftly caught it. It was a battered slug.

"From the coach top," said Dance.

"Burnside?"

Dance nodded.

They looked at each other. "Maybe we ought to go back," said Alec.

"We wouldn't find anything now."

Dance swung up into the driver's seat. Lije Parsons handed Alec a blanket. Bald-headed Greasy, the cook, bustled out and passed up some sandwiches and two cups of coffee. "On the house," he said. "Send the cups back on the next stagecoach."

"Thanks, Greasy," said Alec.

Alec mounted to his seat and wrapped the blanket about his shoulders. Dance emptied his cup quickly and tossed it to Greasy. He drove the stage out onto the road and set off at a steady pace for the next swing station. Alec gnawed at his sandwich. It was good thick beef, covered with Greasy's special hot sauce.

It was midnight when they drove on from the swing station at Sidewinder Well. Alec dozed in his seat. The motion of the coach lulled him. But Dance Birney drove as though he had just got on the driver's seat.

Chapter Twelve

"WAKE UP ALEC!" ALEC OPENED HIS EYES. IT was dawn, and they were crossing the bridge over Yucca Creek. Alec yawned and stretched. He had spelled Dance for a time during the early morning. His arms still ached from handling the team on a rough part of the road.

Dance glanced at the huge bed of ashes and burned timbers where the King Line buildings had once stood. "No use stopping there," he said quietly. He drew the coach to a halt at the office.

Alec dropped to the ground. "I hope we'll hear good news about the new road," he said.

"We will. Alec. We will."

They unharnessed the team and led it to the livery stable. "Let's wake up your father and get some breakfast," said Dance.

Bert King was up when they entered the house. "I don't have to ask you if you got the coach," he said. "I can tell by the looks on your ugly faces."

"Is that bacon I smell?" asked Dance.

"It is, and I have a dozen fresh eggs. How many, Dance?"

"Put in the whole dozen. Alec and I are good for five apiece."

While they ate, Bert King told them about the new road. "George Barren is rebuilding Tonto Pass station. Dan Packard has reached Cuchillo Peak. Ory Carter is at work at Black Rock swing station and will finish Cactus Spring as well. We are planning a better and bigger corral at Stony Creek station. There is plenty of timber there for the building of a temporary station. The army has okay'd our using an abandoned block-house at Lone Hill for a swing station. I've already sent out some coach horses and have arranged for more stock on loan from Joe Simmons."

"*¡Bueno!*" said Dance. "What does Corson think of all this?"

Bert's face darkened. "He's taking bets all over town and giving odds that we don't open the new run in time."

"Maybe I ought to take him up on it."

"Don't do it! There are a lot of chestnuts to be pulled from the fire yet."

"If we only had a few more coaches."

"Ed Schmidt has been working steadily on one of our older coaches that was out in the yard behind the wagon shed. It's somewhat rickety, but Ed is doing the best he can."

"How about forage?"

"There is grazing near most of the new stations,

and I've already sent out dry forage to the stations that need it the most."

"Who drives on the first run?"

Alec's father grinned. "Now that's a silly question to ask, Dance."

"Thanks, Bert."

"I don't know whether I'm doing you a favor or not. The Tontos have been quiet, but there's no telling what they might be up to. You know how they are."

Dance nodded. He reached for his hat and showed the bullet hole to Bert. Alec's father paled. "Where did this happen?"

"Owl Pass."

"Apaches?"

Dance shook his head. "I'll bet this hat against a month's wages it wasn't."

"Then who could it be?"

"We'll find out. And when we *do* find out…"

Bert nodded. "We haven't time now to fool around looking for dirty dry-gulches."

Dance threw the slug he had dug out from the coach roof onto the table. "Burnside," he said.

"Finding a man with a Burnside in this country shouldn't be too hard. Even if we did find a man who carried one, it's no proof that he did the shooting at our coaches."

"No."

There was a shrill whistle outside.

Bert King smiled. "That's Denny. His folks came back. He's been pestering me ever since you left, trying to find out when you'd be back."

Alec walked outside. Denny was sitting on the top rail of the little corral where Alec sometimes kept Biscuits. The sun shone on Denny's mop of red hair. He beckoned Alec closer. "I might have a lead on that mysterious Burnside," he said.

"Keep talking. Denny."

Denny looked cautiously about as if someone might be listening to them. "My father sent me out to Cahan's Store at Junction to get some tools he left there. You know the store?"

"Certainly. It's crammed so full of stuff you can hardly walk around inside of it."

"Right! Well, while I was waiting for Old Man Cahan to get the tools, I looked around the store. Naturally, I ended up where the guns and cartridges are kept. Lordy, Old Man Cahan has guns in there from the Revolution. I never saw so many. You name it, and he has it."

"Go on," urged Alec.

"Then T looked at the cartridges. Every kind you can think of. I saw a box of Burnside cartridges at the back of the case. When Mr. Cahan came back with the tools, I asked him if he sold many Burnside cartridges. He laughed and told me no. Then he remembered that he had had two boxes in that case, and now there was only one box, so he said his clerk must have sold a box while he was elsewhere. I asked for the clerk, and Mr. Cahan told me it was the clerk's day off but that he'd be back the next day and could tell me who the cartridges were bought by."

Alec nodded. "When do we leave?"

"Maybe you're too tired to go."

"Me? I'm all right. I'll tell Dad we're going over to Junction to look at something or other."

"Wait while I get my cayuse."

Alec was waiting for Denny when Dance came out of the King house. "Why are you really going to Junction?" he asked.

Alec smiled mysteriously. "I'll tell you when we get back."

Denny rode up. "Let's go, Alec."

Dance watched them ride out to the road. He shrugged and went back into the house.

———

JUNCTION WAS HARDLY MORE than a motley collection of adobe houses, jacal shacks made of poles thrust into the ground and plastered with clay and a few frame houses. The little hamlet was three miles from Yucca Flats. It seemed to be sleeping in the sun. Cahan's General Emporium dominated the little settlement. Alec and Denny entered the store. A spring bell tinkled as the door was opened.

The interior was a jungle of sacks, bales, boxes, barrels, and tubs. Pots, pans, skillets, spiders, and grills hung from wires stretched from one side of the dusty store to the other. Saddles, bridles, *reatas*, spurs, and boots were racked at one side. The air was redolent with the mingled odors of candy, molasses, kerosene, leather, spices, and cheeses.

Denny walked back to the section of the store

where carbines, shotguns, rifles, and pistols were racked. There was a long dust-covered glass case in front of the guns filled with holsters, cleaning rods, bar lead, shot, powder containers, primers, wads, and boxed cartridges of all calibers.

Denny placed a finger atop the case. "See," he whispered. He indicated a box of cartridges labeled Burnside Carbine Cartridges Caliber .54.

"Howdy, boys."

The cracked voice startled Alec. He looked up to see Old Man Cahan. Moses Cahan was a fixture in Junction. There wasn't anything he didn't know about general-store merchandise. Anyone who couldn't find some obsolete or long-forgotten item in the three general stores in Yucca Flats would ride out to Junction and ask Moses Cahan. There weren't many times when Moses couldn't poke about in the dusty recesses of his big store and find the very item.

Denny smiled. "You said you'd tell me who bought that other box of Burnside cartridges, Mr. Cahan."

"So I did. Why do you want to know?"

Denny shrugged. "Just curious, is all."

Moses Cahan closed one eye. "So?"

"My dad used to have a Burnside," lied Denny. "He wants to buy another one. He thought the man who bought those cartridges might want to sell his."

"H'mmm. You sure you two boys ain't Pinkerton detectives looking for a road agent?"

"Nope," said Denny. "We ain't."

"Wells Fargo agents?"

"Nope."

"US marshals?" persisted Moses.

"Nope."

"Maybe postal inspectors?"

"No," said Denny. "We're a couple of deputy sheriffs."

"That's better. I'll get Eb." Moses Cahan walked into the back room of the store. "Eb! Couple of deputies looking for you."

"I ain't done nothing, Moses."

"Well, anyway, you'd better talk to them. They look hard-case to me. They want to know about them Burnside cartridges you sold a while back."

A little hook-nosed man came out of the back room. "That all you boys want to know?"

"Yep," said Denny.

Eb leaned on the counter. "Lemme see. He was a big man. Not tall, you understand, but big of bone, with solid meat on him. Had a broad face and green eyes. Hard them eyes were, like glass. He gave me the creeps, he did. Wore a black hat. Levi trousers tucked into flat-heeled boots. Gray-flannel shirt and a cowhide vest. Wore a Remington six-shooter at his left side for a cross-arm draw. Didn't talk much."

"Thanks," said Denny.

"You know him?" asked Eb.

Denny opened his mouth, but Alec kicked him on the ankle. "No," said Denny.

Eb eyed them steadily. "Well, I got to finish unpacking some goods. Hope I helped you. You might find him in Yucca Flats. He didn't come from Junction." Eb shuffled into the back room.

The boys walked outside and mounted. They rode to the edge of town and then looked at each other. "Rig Conboy," they said at the same time.

Alec shoved back his hat. "Doesn't really mean anything," he said.

"Nope."

Alec looked at Denny. "You said you wanted to get a Burnside for your father. What if Moses had one in there?"

Denny grinned. "I remembered I didn't see one in the store the last time I was there."

"Where does Rig Conboy live in town?"

"In the hotel."

Alec slapped a hand down on his thigh. "We'll take a look in his room tonight. I don't ever remember seeing him carry a Burnside saddle gun."

"Me neither."

They rode quickly back toward Yucca Flats.

Chapter Thirteen

ALEC HAD BEEN KEPT BUSY ALL AFTERNOON running errands for his father. Bert King's office was a beehive of work. Men came and went. The time was drawing close for the completion of the new road, and many things had to be thought about and arranged. Ed Schmidt inspected the coach that Dance and Alec had brought in from Yavapai Wells and made a few minor repairs. Dance occupied his time at Joe Simmon's Livery Stable, matching up teams of horses for the new run. Three wagonloads of supplies under the charge of Bartolome Madera left Yucca Flats to replenish stocks at the new stations.

It was nine o'clock at night before Alec had any free time to himself. His father was still at the office. Alec and Denny walked down the alleyway that was behind the hotel.

"Rig Conboy is at the Beacon," said Denny. "I looked at his saddle gun. It's a Henry rifle."

Alec stopped at the rear of the hotel and peered in

through the murky glass of the back door. The long corridor was empty, but he knew that Neal Peters, the night clerk, would be on duty at the desk just beyond the end of the corridor. Alec tested the door. It squeaked. He stepped back as he saw Neal enter the corridor and walk swiftly toward the rear door. The two boys faded into the darkness and hid behind a huge rain barrel.

The door squeaked open. "Funny," said Xeal Peters, "I thought sure I heard this door open." He closed it.

Denny shook his head. "Xeal Peters can hear like an Apache," he said. "My father says he got that way from listening for hotel guests who were trying to sneak out without paying their bills."

"No use trying that door again. I wish we knew what room was Rig Conboy's."

"That's easy. Number Six, second floor, on the south side."

"How'd you find out?"

Denny grinned. "I wasn't doing chores *all* day, Sonny."

Alec looked up. "If we stand on that shed roof, we can reach the railing of the second-floor rear porch."

"*¡Sí!*"

They climbed atop the shed and pulled themselves up over the porch railing. No lights snowed from the rear windows. Alec eased open the hotel door. The corridor was dimly lit. The two boys padded down the corridor to Number Six and tried the door. It was locked.

"Maybe he left his window open," said Denny.

They walked back to the rear porch and followed it to the south side of the building. The side porch overlooked Cottonwood Street. The street was deserted. They walked softly past a lighted window and then found the window of Number Six. It was closed. Alec took out his sheath knife and slid the tip under the lower sash. He pried up and the window gave a little. He and Denny raised the window.

Denny looked into the dark interior. "Who's first?"

Alec did not answer. He stepped into the room. Denny hesitated and then followed him. Alec looked about. As his eyes got accustomed to the darkness, he could make out the brass bedstead, a marble-topped dresser, and a huge wardrobe closet. "Pull down the shade," he said.

Denny pulled down the shade as he was bid. Alec lit a match and held it up. He ignited the Argand lamp that stood on a small table and turned the flame down low. Clothing was scattered about the room. A pair of dusty boots lay near the door. There was some loose change, a cheap watch, a tobacco pouch, and a pocket case of matches on the dresser.

Denny eased open the wardrobe door. He pawed through the clothing hanging in there. "Whew!" he said. "Old Rig sure could use a washerwoman on these duds."

"Look for a Burnside carbine."

"Ain't none in here."

Alec prowled about the room. He looked under the bed and then under the lumpy mattress.

"Any luck?" asked Denny.

"No."

Denny raised his head. "Listen," he said. "Footsteps on the stairs!"

"Beat it!"

Denny ran to the window and climbed out on the porch. Alec put out the lamp and started for the window. As he did so, he heard the metallic noise of a key being inserted into the door lock. There was no time to make it to the window. Alec stepped into the wardrobe and pulled the door shut behind him. He heard the room door bang back against the wall as he felt his way back behind the musty-smelling clothing. Denny had been right. Rig Conboy sure needed a washerwoman.

Heavy steps sounded in the room. "Set a minute, Monk," said Rig Conboy.

"Don't take too long, Rig."

"Corson can wait. He's kept me so blasted busy I ain't had much chance to loaf a little."

"You should gripe about being kept busy. Ross pays you plenty."

"He'd better. I got enough on Ross Corson to send him to the *calabozo* for twenty years."

Alec was almost stifled in the musty, sour-smelling wardrobe.

"All the same," said Monk, "if Corson thought you'd do any talking, you'd end up in an unmarked grave out in the desert."

Conboy laughed. "Oh, I ain't goin' to talk. Besides, he needs me too much."

"You still driving for him?"

"Naw! I got more important jobs to do."

"Such as?"

"Don't get nosy, Monk."

"I was just wondering."

"Well, keep on wonderin'. We got some hard riding to do tonight."

"Which way?"

"North."

"Why does Corson want me to go with you?"

"You speak Tonto, don't you?"

"Enough to get by."

"That's why Ross wants you to go with me."

"I don't care much for this business."

Rig laughed. "You'll get paid enough for the job. We'll meet some of the boys at Lopez Seep."

Alec's heart seemed to thud against his chest as the wardrobe door was jerked open. His throat went dry. A big hand pawed through the clothing inches from his nose. Once the hand barely touched his left cheek. Conboy took out some clothing but left the door open. Alec hoped the big man wouldn't look down and see Alec's feet below the concealing clothing.

Feet shuffled on the floor. "Put out the light. Monk," said Rig Conboy.

The light went out, and the door was shut and locked. Alec took a deep breath, but he stayed where he was until he heard the noise of footsteps die away on the stairs. Sweat trickled icily down Alec's sides, and he felt uneasy in his stomach from fear and the stench of Conboy's filthy clothing.

"Alec! Alec!" It was Denny calling from the window.

Alec stepped forward. His right foot caught on something, and he fell through the doorway to sprawl on the floor.

"What's the matter, Alec?" asked Denny hoarsely.

"Nothing." Alec removed the entangling strap from his right ankle. He stood up. "There's no use in staying here." He lit a match.

"What's that thing on the floor?"

Alec picked it up. A buckskin bag hung at the end of a looped strap. Alec lit another match and opened the bag. He examined the contents. "A lot of junk," he said. Then he stared at a small clay pot. The lid had come off it. It was full of a whitish substance. It looked like war paint.

"What is it?"

"How should I know? Let's get out of here."

Alec threw the bag back into the wardrobe. They lowered the window and returned to the alley.

"Fine thing," said Denny. "We didn't learn anything."

"I don't know about that. Rig Conboy and that man with him are going somewhere."

"Yeh. I heard most of their talk. Don't mean anything."

Alec looked at his friend. "They're going somewhere where they have to know how to talk Tonto, well at least Monk has to know."

"North, they said."

Alec nodded. "Up in Diabolito's country."

Denny whistled softly. "Something sneaky going on, do you think?"

"I'm willing to bet on it. Let's go find my father and Dance Bimey."

Alec's father and Dance were in the office going over a list of required supplies for the new line. They listened to Alec's story. Bert King shook his head. "I thought you two boys would be safe in town. Now I'm beginning to think you'd be better off in the Grindstone Hills."

"But don't you see, Mr. King?" cried Denny. "Rig Conboy must have a Burnside carbine *somewhere*. Maybe it was him that did the dry-gulching in Owl Pass."

"And maybe it wasn't, Denny."

Dance tilted his chair back against the wall. You boys haven't proved Rig had anything to do with the shooting in Owl Pass. What puzzles me, though, is this business of him riding north with Monk Dorn."

"You know this man Monk then?" asked Alec's father.

Dance nodded. "He used to trade with the Tontos. The type of trader they call Comancheros in Texas. They'd trade liquor and guns for anything of value the Indians had. The Indians left them alone because of that."

"That explains how Monk knows Tonto," said Alec.

"Has he been around town lately?" asked Bert King.

"No," said Dance. "He keeps to himself. He's the sort of *hombre* who'd sell his grandmother to make a profit."

"Where is Lopez Seep?" asked Alec.

Dance stood up and walked to the wall map. He placed a finger on the map. "Here, west of Tonto Pass, close to the area where Diabolito is supposed to have his camp. Why do you ask?"

"Because that's where Rig Conboy and Monk Dorn were heading."

Dance whirled. "Bert, I'll bet Conboy has something to do with the Tontos' getting new repeating rifles. I wouldn't put it past Corson to have Conboy do such a thing. I'll pull out of here as soon as I can and head for Lopez Seep to see if I can find out what they're doing in there."

Bert King shook his head. "I can't let you go off on a wild-goose chase. You're going to drive the first coach over the new division to Tres Cabezas."

Dance planted both hands on Bert King's desk. "Don't you see we might get a lead on these men? We might find out that Corson is behind the gunrunning that has been going on. Let me go, Bert!"

Alec's father stood up. "Listen, Dance, I'm running a stage line, not an investigation bureau. I've got to get that first coach through to Tres Cabezas in time, and you're the man who's going to do it for me."

Dance straightened up. "All right, Bert."

Alec's father looked at the two boys. "And as for you two, don't get any foolhardy ideas of sneaking off to Lopez Seep. You understand? You've risked your necks twice now, and you'll not get a chance to do it again."

Alec nodded. Denny grinned. "Why, Mr. King, we had no idea of going to Lopez Seep. Did we, Alec?"

"No."

Bert King put out the lamp. "We'd all better get some sleep. There's only a short time left to finish preparations for the initial run to Tres Cabezas. We can't leave anything to chance."

They walked up the moonlit street. Alec looked north toward the Grindstone Hills. Their lead on Rig Conboy had petered out. Now Rig Conboy was somewhere in those hills on some mysterious business, accompanied by an unscrupulous man who spoke Tonto.

"I wish we were five years older," whispered Denny. "We could follow Rig Conboy and maybe foil his plans."

"You've been reading dime novels again," said Alec. He thought of the time he had rescued Mike Tagger from Owl Pass. It was then he had found the buckskin bag of *hoddentin* that should have proved that the job had been done by Apaches. But Dance had insisted that the Apaches would not go near Owl Pass. Yet there had been three attacks on King Line stage-coaches in the pass.

Mike Tagger hadn't seen any Apaches. He had assumed his ambushers had been Apaches. Charley Lee had died at Cabatlo swing station without identifying his attackers. When Dance and Alec had been ambushed, they had not actually seen who had fired upon them.

Alec wondered about the buckskin bag he had found in Rig Conboy's room. He opened his mouth to speak to his father and then he thought better of it. Bert King was in no mood to conjecture about buckskin bags. He was completely concerned about getting his Tres Ca-bezas division open in order to save his mail franchise.

Later, after Alec had gone to bed, he lay awake, staring at the ceiling. Dance would leave for Tres Cabezas the day after next. There wouldn't be anything for Alec to do but sit in Yucca Flats and wait to hear whether Dance had got through or not. It would be a thrill to sit beside Dance Bimey as he drove his Concord through to Tres Cabezas, but there was no chance of that. A good shotgun messenger would be chosen to accompany Dance. There would be no passengers on the first run.

Alec had thought of asking his father to let him and Denny ride as passengers, but he knew they would not be allowed to go.

Alec was in an awkward age right now—old enough to know the fundamentals of station manager- ship and of coach driving but too young to accept responsibilities. He knew his father had plans for his future, and it would probably be with the King Line, if his father could save the business. The thing that troubled Alec was that his father almost had his back against the wall in his fight to keep the King Line going, and there wasn't very much that he, Alec, could do to help him.

Alec could hear the low voices of Dance Birney and Bert King as they talked in the living room. Dance had been a pillar of strength to his boss. Now, Alec's father relied on the skilled young stagecoach driver to make a successful first run on the new division to save the mail franchise.

Alec closed his eyes. He could envision himself riding beside Dance Birney, first to Black Rock swing station, thence on the long, easy grade to Cactus Spring. He could almost see the narrow, winding road on the way to Stony Creek and then the hazardous road to dread Tonto Pass. Alec imagined sweeping past lofty Cuchillo Peak, then climbing Hogback Ridge to shoot down at breakneck speed to Lone Hill.

What a celebration there would be at Tres Cabezas when the dusty coach, with Dance Birney up and Alec King beside him as shotgun messenger, raced into the town and drew up in front of the company office one minute ahead of the deadline for the mail run!

An owl hooted softly from the big cottonwood outside Alec's window. It was the last thing he remembered.

Chapter Fourteen

ORY CARTER CAME TO THE KING HOUSE AT dawn. He was dead tired, and his face was covered with whiskers, but he brought good news. The road was all the way through to Tres Cabezas. It was very rough in places, but a coach, if properly driven, could make the trip in time.

Alec made coffee as he listened to Ory and Bert talk.

Alec's father sat in his big chair with a pad on his lap, writing notes as Ory spoke. When the tired employee finished, Bert King made a few more notes. He looked up at Ory. "We can average about sixty miles in six hours on a good road. If the new road was as good as the road to Yavapai Wells, we could get a stage through to Tres Cabezas in about ten hours, considering the steeper grades on the new run."

Ory nodded. "Good time can be made from here to Stony Creek. From Stony Creek to Tonto Pass, the pace will be slower. From Tonto Pass to Hogback

Ridge, the pace can't be much more than a fast walk in places. After Hogback Ridge, it's all downhill to Lone Hill and then a fast-level stretch into Tres Cabezas."

Alec's father wrote swiftly. "All things considered," he said, "I think the trip can be made in between eleven and twelve hours. That leaves considerable leeway. We have to figure on rockfalls and the like. You're tired, Ory. I'll send another man with Dance."

Ory shook his head. "I'll be fresh as a daisy when that trip starts. Don't you worry about that. I can spell Dance during the rough spots and let him handle the Concord where we can make the greatest speed. What time do we have to be in Tres Cabezas?"

"I've been given no time limit. All I've been told is that the trip must be completed the day after tomorrow."

"That's one break anyway. You got twenty-four hours for the trip."

"I can't take twenty-four hours for the trip. We've got to make as fast a trip as we can. People won't ride in a coach that is as slow as molasses in January, if they can help it. I want this initial trip to be made in good time, with allowances for any unforeseen eventualities."

"With luck, we'll make a good run."

Bert King looked up. "It will take more than luck. It will take top driving, fast teamwork at the swing stations, and strong, fast teams. I have confidence in my equipment, employees, and horses. Nothing has been left to chance."

Ory nodded. "We'll make it, Bert."

Bert stood up. "I want to be able to letter United States Mail on my coaches. Incidentally, I've been notified that the first coach to Tres Cabezas will carry the payroll for the mining company there. Forty thousand dollars."

Ory whistled softly. "I'd better clean up my shotgun."

"Let's hope you won't have to use it."

Alec served coffee to the two men. He sat down on the couch and looked at Ory. "I wish I could ride shotgun," he said.

Ory grinned. "Your day will come. This run is no place for a kid, Alec."

Alec's father nodded. "Ory," he said, "is there anything else you have to tell me?"

Ory looked down at his cup. "No."

Bert's steady eyes studied Ory. "You're keeping something to yourself."

"Well…I didn't want to say more."

"What are you keeping back?"

Ory drained his cup and placed it on the table. "Tonto scouts have been seen near Tonto Pass station. They haven't bothered the station, but they're always around—just sitting on the heights and watching all the time."

"I was afraid of that."

"Maybe they're just nosy, Bert. Maybe they're waiting for a chance to snap up a horse or mule."

"I hope that's all they're interested in. Rig Conboy and Monk Dorn are somewhere in the Grindstone

Hills. I wouldn't trust either one any more than I would a Tonto."

"Neither would I, but I think Dance and I can take care of those two tinhorn *hombres*."

Ory left for his lodgings. Bert King finished his notes and then went to his office. Alec washed the dishes and gave the house a lick and a promise. The interminable waiting was beginning to wear on him.

Denny Morris looked in at the rear door. "You free?" he asked.

Alec nodded. "There isn't anything for me to do," he said. He put on his hat and walked out into the backyard.

Denny came close to Alec. "I been doing some more undercover work, Alec."

"What have you learned?"

"I was hanging around the hotel early this morning. Neal Peters was having breakfast. I went and got him a newspaper. He was reading about the fire and also about your father's safe being blown open and the money taken. He bought me some breakfast, and we started talking about who might have stolen the money. I worked the conversation around to Rig Conboy and Monk Dora. Then Neal says a funny thing happened the night of the fire. Just about the whole town was out at the fire, he says. He was standing at the front door of the hotel, watching the fire, when he hears the rear door open. He looks back. Rig Conboy was coming up the corridor. He looked surprised when he saw Neal, and then he hurried upstairs."

"So?"

"Rig owed quite a bit of rent. The next morning, he paid his bill just like that without a murmur. Then he went out and bought himself a new horse. Neal was wondering where Rig got all the money."

"That's nothing. He could have got the money anywhere."

"Yeh," said Denny excitedly, "but let me finish. The day clerk was sick and couldn't come to work, so Neal asked me to watch the desk while he got some sleep. I waited until old Xeal was snoring, then I took the key to Number Six and went up to the room. I poked around in there and then got the idea of looking in the trash box in the room. I read about Pinkerton men doing that. It's surprising what they can find out looking in trash boxes."

"I'll bet," said Alec dryly.

"Well, there were empty tobacco sacks, a pair of old socks, some old newspapers in the box."

"Great clues."

"Take it easy, will you? Then I found this." Denny handed Alec some crumpled envelopes.

Alec looked at the envelopes. Some of them had been addressed to people in Yavapai Wells and were postmarked with dates not more than a few weeks old. The last envelope had evidently not contained a letter, for there was no address or postmark on it, but the name "J.C. Riser" was written on it in Alec's father's unmistakable scrawl. Written on the lower left-hand corner was the number "182."

"Let's go to the office," said Alec quickly.

They hurried down the street to the office. Alec's

father and Dance Birncy Were there. Denny told them what he had discovered.

Alec's father looked at the envelope that had his writing on it. "This envelope is from the safe. There was one hundred and eight-two dollars in it, along with a bill I owed John Riser for some sets of harnesses. I was holding it until John returned from Yuma."

Dance picked up the other envelopes. "I wonder where he got these."

"They might have been part of the mail looted at Owl Pass," said Alec. "I'll bet they had money in them too."

Dance nodded. "Fred Horton should see these," he said. "I'll find him." He hurried from the office.

"What are you going to do?" asked Alec of his father.

"Rig Conboy is gone. This envelope of mine is nothing but circumstantial evidence, but it is a start to incriminating Rig Conboy if he did blow my safe. If he is behind the holdups in Owl Pass and it can be proved, he'll spend a good part of his remaining life in jail. Denny, you've got a head on your shoulders. I wouldn't be surprised if you became a Pinkerton detective one of these days."

"It was nothing," said Denny airily.

"Rig Conboy will come back one of these days, and when he does, he will have to answer some questions. It might be that Rig does have a Burnside carbine and that he did use it at Owl Pass. In that case, he'll face charges of murder, too, for the killing of Charley Lee.

You boys have done a fine job. But listen to me: You've taken too many chances already. Now let me handle this from now on."

"All right, Mr. King," said Denny.

The boys whiled away the time inspecting the coach Dance Birney and Ory Carter would drive on the initial run to Tres Cabezas. Ed Schmidt came out to the coach as they finished their inspection. "She's in good shape," said Ed. "I've re-enforced the running gear here and there. The only thing I'm worried about is the fact that metal sometimes gets worn and will snap when you least expect it to. That's something I can't foresee, though. I haven't time to give the coach as thorough an overhauling as I'd like to."

"She'll be all right," said Denny.

"Let's hope so," said Ed.

It was after eleven o'clock when they went back to the office. Fred Horton and Dance Birney entered the office right behind them.

"I think we've got something on Rig Conboy," said Fred. "I tracked down the three people to whom these letters were addressed. One of them was a man who has been expecting a letter from his brother with money in it. One was a woman who thought sure her husband had mailed a letter to her from Tucson with money in it. The third person was a man who didn't know whether he had any money coming to him or not, but he sometimes gets checks made out to cash from his business partner in Tombstone."

"Well," said Alec's father, "do you have enough

evidence to charge Rig Conboy with robbing the mails?"

"We have enough to start proceedings. Where is Conboy?"

"Up in the Grindstone Hills with Monk Horn."

"That's a great help. But I'll notify the sheriff in Yavapai Wells as quickly as I can. Dance said Denny had found a letter from your safe in Conboy's room."

"That's right."

"You think Conboy might have robbed your safe?"

"I'm almost sure of it."

"I'll bet on it," said Dance quietly.

Fred Horton took the letters and placed them in his pocket. "I'll get on this right away. Another thing is Bert,I've got some bad news for you."

"So?"

"Ross Corson put on a little pressure through a friend of his in the Territorial Legislature at Tucson. I've received instructions to the effect that you must deliver your first load of mail in Tres Cabezas no later than four o'clock tomorrow afternoon."

Bert King looked up quickly. "Four o'clock? My original instructions were that the delivery could be made any time tomorrow!"

Fred Horton flushed. "It's none of my doing, Bert. The good Lord knows I want you to keep the franchise. I have no use for Ross Corson or for his political friends in Tucson, but I get my orders from my superior. I'd be willing to give you a full week to get the mail through. You've done a fine job in getting that road done. You've faced great odds by losing your coaches in that fire. All I can do now is wish you the best of luck."

"Thanks, Fred."

The postal inspector left the office. Bert King stood up and began to pace back and forth. "Four o'clock," he said. "It's a fine thing when a man like Corson can influence the Post Office Department."

Dance eyed the route map on the wall. "If I pull out of here no later than four a.m., I can make it. Supposing I leave here one minute after midnight? That would give me sixteen hours for the trip."

"No! I aim to make this as fast a trip as I can. You'll leave here at four a.m. sharp. We'll show Corson that the King Line isn't licked yet."

"It could have been worse," said Dance. "They might have told you to get the mail in Tres Cabezas by noon."

"Thank God for small favors!"

Dance nodded. "I can hardly wait until I get back here and get my hands on Rig Conboy."

"That makes two of us, Dance."

Bert King stopped at his desk. "Let's get cracking," he said. "Every last-minute detail must be checked and rechecked. The teams are hand-picked. The stations are ready for you. I only wish the road were in better shape."

"I've driven over worse roads, Bert."

The day passed swiftly after that. Alec almost ran his legs off on last-minute details. The payroll chest was delivered from the bank. The mail sacks were piled up in the office. An employee was detailed to guard the payroll and the mailbags. Bert King assigned other employees to stand guard-shifts throughout the night. Alec was given the job of cleaning and loading a company shotgun for Ory Carter's use. He cleaned the twin barrels until they glistened. Then he loaded them and placed the shotgun near the office door. Two Spencers were also to be taken along as armament. The two drivers would have their Colts as well.

Alec, his father, and Dance had dinner in the restaurant. Bert King could hardly eat, but Alec and Dance did full justice to the meal.

"You'd better eat, Bert," advised Dance.

"I've lost my appetite for the first time in my life. It seems hard to realize that the whole future of the King Line depends on that mail run tomorrow."

"Ory and I will make it, Bert."

They finished their meal and walked toward the office. Ross Corson was riding a fine black up the street. He drew rein and looked down at them. "Tomorrow's the big day, eh, King?" he asked.

"You know that. Thanks for getting me that four o'clock deadline."

Ross Corson smiled. "I like things done right. My coaches keep a tight schedule, so why shouldn't yours?"

"They will."

"We'll see. If you don't make it, King, I'll give you a fair price for your rundown equipment."

"I'll bet you will," said Dance dryly.

Alec had noted that Ross Corson's saddlebags were well-filled. A Winchester repeater was cased in a handsome leather scabbard under Corson's right thigh. He was dressed in trail clothing.

Dance had noted things, too. "Taking a trip, Corson?" he asked.

Corson nodded. "I'm going on to Tres Cabezas to wait and see you miss your deadline, Birney."

"Rather late to be starting out, isn't it? There are Tontos in the hills. Perhaps that doesn't bother you."

Corson flushed. "What do you mean by that?"

Dance smiled coldly. "Nothing. Most men wouldn't pass through those hills at night unless they were sure they were safe from the Tontos."

Corson rested his hand on his thigh close to the holstered pistol he wore. "You talk a lot, Birney," he said thinly. "Too much for your age."

Dance moved away from Alec and Bert. "I'm old enough to face you down. Corson."

Bert King stepped in between them. "Come on, Dance," he said. "This is no time for personal grudges."

Ross Corson laughed. He spurred his horse. He looked back as he rode. "I won't bother with you. Birney," he called back. "I'm almost sure the Tontos will take care of you tomorrow."

Dance started forward, but Bert King held him back. "Enough!" he snapped.

"All right, Bert. All right."

Later, as Alec got ready for bed, he thought of Ross Corson's last words. He felt sure that Ross Corson was behind anything Rig Conboy had done to harm the King Line. Alec plainly remembered the conversation between Rig Conboy and Monk Dorn in Rig's hotel room. Rig had hinted strongly that Ross Corson wasn't averse to crooked dealings. They might try to stop the mail coach from going through, and dead men could tell no tales. Alec laid out his trail clothing and checked his Sharps and Colt. A plan had formed in his mind.

Chapter Fifteen

IT WAS TWO O'CLOCK IN THE MORNING WHEN Alec left the house. He carried his Sharps and a canteen. Alec shivered in the cold wind as he hurried toward the office. The office was lighted, and a man sat in a chair, with a shotgun across his lap, guarding the mail and the payroll chest.

Alec unbuckled the straps of the rear boot cover. The boot was empty. Alec knew that the mail and the payroll chest were to be carried inside the coach to keep the weight better balanced. Alec climbed into the boot and pulled down the cover. It was cold and he would be cramped, but he made himself as comfortable as possible. He was dozing when he heard voices outside the coach.

"Let's load up. Ory," said Dance.

Hoofs thudded on the street as the team was brought up. The coach door was opened as the team was being harnessed, and the cargo was stowed inside the coach. Footsteps sounded on the board sidewalk and then the office door slammed shut.

Something scraped on the canvas boot cover. Alec held his breath. Then the cover was pulled back, and a questioning hand felt about inside the boot. The hand struck Alec's right ankle and then worked up to his knee and stopped there. Alec looked out into the homely face of Denny Morris. "I might have known it would be you," hissed Alec. "You want to ruin everything? Beat it."

"I figured you'd be in here."

"Well, here I am. Now beat it!"

Denny grinned. "If you're going along, then so am I."

"There isn't enough room."

"There is under the mailbags."

"They'll find you."

"Oh, no, they won't."

Alec shook his head. He hadn't figured on Denny's getting the same idea he had thought up.

Denny withdrew his hand. "See you later," he said. "I left a note where my ma could find it, telling her where I'd gone."

"If she finds it, we'll be discovered!"

"She won't get up until six. We'll be gone two hours by then." Denny vanished from Alec's sight. A moment later, Alec heard the left-hand coach door open. The coach sagged a little as Denny got in. Then Alec heard a scuffling among the mailbags.

The office door opened. Boots thudded on the boardwalk. A man walked around the coach. "Blasted fools didn't strap down the boot," said Dance Birney, so close to Alec that Alec felt he could reach out and touch him. The straps were buckled tight.

The coach sagged and swayed a little.

"All set, Dance?" called out Bert King.

"As set as I'll ever be."

"Don't worry, Bert," said Ory Carter. "We'll make it on time."

There was a moment's pause, and then the brake was released. Dance's whip cracked like a pistol shot, and the coach rolled forward and gathered speed. Alec settled back in the swaying boot.

"Good luck!" called out Bert King.

The coach swayed a little as it cut across some ruts and it picked up more speed as Dance let out the team. The hoofs sounded hollowly as the team crossed a wooden bridge, and Alec knew they were on the open road, heading for Black Rock swing station on the first leg of the vital trip to Tres Cabezas.

Alec slid a hand between the canvas cover and the boot side and loosened some of the buckles. He pulled the flap back and looked out on the dim road. Here and there in Yucca Flats, he could see lighted windows as early risers prepared for the day's work.

———

THE COACH MADE good time to Black Rock swing station. The noise of the men changing teams came clearly to Alec. He had pulled the cover flap down tight, hoping Dance would not notice the loose straps.

It took ten minutes to change the team, and then the Concord shot out onto the road for the fifteen-mile stage to Cactus Spring.

Alec was cramped and miserable in his narrow hiding place. The sun was up, but it was still cold. He shifted as much as he could, but it seemed as if the bolt heads that protruded from the boot floor were determined to drill holes right through him. He pumped his head and cracked an elbow as the coach crossed a rocky gully. Dust seeped into the boot, and he coughed and sneezed continually. Denny was better off than he was, and was probably asleep under the mailbags.

When the coach stopped at Cactus Spring, Alec was almost ready to give himself up, but the team was changed and the coach went on, climbing the long, rough ascent toward Stony Creek. The sun was up now, and it was getting warmer inside the boot. The coach swayed and bounced as it made the climb. Alec unbuckled all the cover straps on one side and stood up. He pulled himself up to look across the coach top. Ory Carter was driving. Dance's head turned from side to side, watching the border of the road for possible trouble. Alec sat down and hung his legs out of the back of the boot. He retreated to the interior of the boot when the coach neared Stony Creek swing station for another team change.

The coach was driven on from Stony Creek up the long grade into Tonto Pass. Dust swirled up from the rear wheels and coated Alec thickly. The road was narrow and winding and full of chuckholes. A mile from Tonto Pass station, the team was halted. Alec quickly pulled down the boot cover.

"That's a lot of smoke for just a breakfast fire," said Ory Carter. "Right, Dance?"

"Yen," said Dance. "But there's no use in staying here, Ory."

The coach went on and then halted again. Alec poked out his head. The Concord had been stopped on the road just below the rise upon which Tonto Pass home station stood. A bitter cloud of smoke drifted over the coach. Alec craned his neck to see the station. What he saw made him sick.

A man lay face downward close beside the road. Blood stained the back of his head. There was no doubt that he was dead. The horses were shying and blowing. The stone station house was blackened with smoke, and the wooden roof had fallen in. It was burning steadily inside the big building. Another man lay in front of the station house. His hands clutched his bloody shirt front, and his sightless eyes stared up at the sky.

Dance Birncy came into Alec's line of vision. He held his Spencer in his hands as he walked toward the station house. He passed behind it. A few minutes later, he returned. "Two more of them dead behind the building, Ory!" he called.

"Apaches!"

"Looks like it. There's not a horse anywhere in sight."

"What do we do now?"

Dance looked back at the burning station house. "We go on," he said.

Dance came down the slope. Alec ducked back into the boot, but Dance had seen him.

"Come on out, kid!" he said.

"Who you talking to, Dance?" yelled Oiy.

"Alec King. He's in the boot."

"The little lunkhead!"

Alec gripped his Sharps and then slid to the ground. He looked at Dance. Dance raised his hand as if to strike Alec, and then he shook his head and dropped his hand. "What's the use?" he said.

"I didn't want anything to happen to you, Dance," said Alec quietly.

"You might as well bawl me out, too," said Denny Morris from the coach window.

Dance whirled. "You too? What are we running here? A ride for school kids?"

Denny opened the door and got out. Then he saw the dead man beside the road. Denny paled beneath his freckles.

Ory Carter came back to Dance. He looked at the two boys. "Well, you're here now." He pointed at the dead man with his carbine. "Take a good look, and you'll see what you've let yourself in for."

Dance looked at the quiet hills. "I have a feeling we're being watched right now. But these two boys can shoot. Maybe they'll have to show how well they can shoot before we get out of these hills. Get inside the coach, boys."

Alec fastened down the rear flap and then got into

the coach with Denny. Denny shivered a little. "This isn't going to be any picnic, Alec," he said quietly.

Dance drove the team past the station. The odor of burning wood hung in the pass until they were a good mile from the station.

"Where do we go from here?" asked Denny.

"Thirty miles into Tres Cabezas. The next swing station is at Lone Hill, fifteen miles from here."

The sun beat down on the hills as the coach rolled along. There was no sign of life on the gaunt, tree-stippled heights, but it was as Dance had said, and there was a feeling of being watched.

———

THEY WATERED the tired team at a little stream that flowed across the road. Alec and Denny stood guard, eyeing the heights with wary eyes. Dance inspected the coach's running gear. "Okay," he said. "We'll rest the team for half an hour. Get out some food, Ory."

They gnawed at thick sandwiches, but their eyes were on the silent hills. The road ahead of them was narrow and rough. Dan Packard had smoothed out the worst places, but the road was no place to make speed on.

Alec finished his sandwich and then climbed up on a huge rockfall to look north. The country ahead was a veritable maze of jumbled rock and was blanketed thickly by brush and scrub trees. The Tontos could form an ambush anywhere within the next five miles and be unseen until they opened fire. Alec looked down toward the coach. There seemed to be a brooding quietness about the narrow pass. The wind soughed through the trees and brush and moaned about the heights.

Alec came down the slope.

"See anything?" asked Dance.

"No."

"It's too quiet to suit me," said Ory. He drank deeply from his canteen. "I feel like a prime target sitting up on that seat."

Dance nodded. "Everything in me wants me to race out of here as fast as I can, but the horses need rest."

"We'll get a fresh team at Lone Hill, Dance."

"Yeh."

Alec looked quickly at Dance. "You don't suppose…"

Dance shrugged. "I'm supposing nothing," he said quietly.

Denny wiped his damp face. "I wish I was back home."

"I wish you were too," said Ory angrily. "For that matter, I wish I was back home too."

"Shut up," said Dance. "No use in getting excited."

"It ain't easy to be calm," said Ory. "I wish we had a dozen of the boys with us. Like we had when we ambushed Diabolito's bucks."

"A company of cavalry wouldn't stand a chance out on this road," said Dance.

Ory nodded. He walked over to the horses and began to examine their hoofs.

Dance felt in the pocket of his buckskin jacket. He took out three empty cartridge cases and held them out toward the two boys. "Burnsides," he said. "I found them out behind the station house, along with quite a few empty Winchester cases."

"You think it might be the same man who shot up the coaches in Owl Pass?" asked Alec.

"*¿Quién sabe?*"

The boys looked at each other.

"We'd better get rolling," said Dance.

The coach pulled out with Dance on the driver's box. Alec rested his Sharps on a windowsill. He looked back at Denny. Denny was busy piling up mailbags as a sort of improvised breastwork.

"Go easy on the US mail," said Alec.

Denny turned. "A few bullet holes won't hurt these letters, Alec, but if I get killed, my stepfather will wale the daylights out of me."

Alec couldn't help laughing. Denny began to laugh, too.

"Loco kids," growled Ory Carter. "Listen to 'em."

"Let them laugh," said Dance. "It'll keep their minds off the Tontos...for a little while anyway."

Chapter Sixteen

THE CONCORD BUMPED OVER A ROCKFALL and then suddenly sagged over toward the right side. Dance drew in the team. They were in a sort of valley that cut across the narrow road. Alec got out of the coach and looked under it. "Thoroughbrace is stretching," he said.

Dance got down and looked at it. One of the thick folds of leather had parted, weakening the rest of the great leather support for the coach. "Can't make any speed with that thoroughbrace like that," he said.

They worked quickly. The bottom of the coach was supported by rocks, taking the strain from the thoroughbrace. Dance got some tough rawhide thongs and wet them with water from his canteen. He and Alec bound them tightly about the thoroughbrace while Denny and Ory stood guard.

Now and then, Alec looked nervously over his shoulder. It was getting late, and they weren't making much time on the road. They had yet to leave the pass and then drive below the steep slopes of Cuchillo Peak, which loomed to the north.

Alec wiped the sweat from his face and then saw the cracked spoke in the right rear wheel. He showed it to Dance. Dance took another thong and wet it. They bound it tightly about the spoke.

"When that rawhide dries it will draw up tighter," said Dance. "Good thing you spotted that crack. I'd hate to lose a wheel in this place."

"Look!" called out Ory.

They looked in the direction to which he was pointing. Something was flashing from a craggy butte. Then, far across the valley, came an answering flash of light.

"Apaches," said Dance. "Signaling with mirrors."

"There's another mirror flashing," said Denny hoarsely. He pointed to the north.

Dance wiped his hands on his jacket. "The orchestra is tuning up for the dance," he said.

"These horses won't be able to do much dancing," said Ory. "They're getting plumb tuckered out."

"They'll have to do," said Dance.

They eased the coach down off the rocks. The coach sagged a little on the weakened thoroughbrace. "We'll shift the mailbags to the other side," said Dance.

Alec and Denny shifted the bags.

Dance walked around the coach. "I think she'll be all right now."

Dance took the reins, and they moved on. Alec could see the mirrors flashing on the heights, but he could not see the Tontos who were signaling with them. It gave him an eerie feeling.

The Concord bumped and swayed on the rough road. "I hope that thoroughbrace holds up," said Denny.

"It better," said Alec quietly.

It was getting along toward half past one when they reached the first spurs of Cuchillo Peak. The weary horses could hardly move faster than a trot, but Dance kept them at it, letting them walk now and then to ease the strain.

Alec supported himself by a straphanger and looked out the window at the massive Cuchillo Peak. There was no sign of life on the rough slopes. The gaunt peak thrust itself up against the clear blue sky like a warning finger.

Denny felt in his pocket and drew out a little double-barreled derringer pistol. He opened it and inspected the cartridges. "Took it from my pa's dresser," he said.

"What are you going to do with it? *Throw* it at a Tonto?"

Denny closed the little gun. "No," he said quietly, "but they won't take me alive."

Alec had nothing to say. He knew the rule. Save the last cartridge for yourself if you were trapped. It was a hard country, and it had hard rules. He furtively felt the butt of his Colt.

They were halfway past Cuchillo Peak when they reached a dip in the road. Dance slowed the team to a walk to ease the weakened coach across the dip. There was the sound of a breaking stick from the slopes of Cuchillo Peak, and a puff of smoke seemed to blossom from the brush. There was a hoarse cry from Ory Carter that was drowned out by a staccato ripple of gunfire from the slopes.

Alec aimed his Sharps at the brush and fired at a puff of smoke. The crashing discharge of the carbine in the confined interior of the coach nearly deafened Alec. Smoke swirled out of the windows as Dance lashed the weary team into a run.

Denny fired as Alec reloaded. The two boys fired until their carbines were hot. One of the horses screamed like a frightened woman. The coach raced past a naked shoulder of rock. Slugs rapped into it. Another scream came from a horse, and the team lost stride.

"G'lang! G'lang! Hiyup! Hiyup! G'lang!" shrieked Dance as he snapped his long lash over the straining team.

Alec threw down his Sharps, opened the door, and reached up to the roof of the coach. Denny gripped Alec's belt as Alec fought for a hold on the top railing. Then he had it. He placed a foot on a front window sill and pulled himself atop the swaying coach. Ory Carter sagged in his seat, gripping his right shoulder. Blood ran down his hand.

Alec worked his way forward and held on to the wounded man just as the coach rocked perilously. Ory swayed sideways with the motion of the coach, but Alec hung on like grim death.

Up ahead, a barricade of rocks and logs lay across

the narrow road. A shallow stream bordered the road. Dance had no choice. He turned the leaders toward the stream. The nimble little leaders plunged into the water. Spray flew back toward the coach, soaking the three outside riders. Hoofs grated on the gravelly bed of the stream. Guns rattled steadily from the rocks across the road, and slugs slapped into the coach.

The coach bounced back and forth on its thorough-braces as Dance tooled the team back up the bank of the stream. There was a sharp crack from under the coach. One of the big wheel horses stumbled and went part way down, but he was up again and slamming into his collar without hardly missing a stride.

Alec pushed Ory to one side and snatched up Ory's Spencer. He raised it to his shoulder and fired until the stubby repeater was empty.

The shooting faded away behind them as they raced along the rough road. Ory opened his eyes. "I never seen a thing," he said. Then he fainted dead away.

Two miles beyond the ambush, Dance slowed the team to a walk and then drew it to a halt. Alec reloaded the Spencer and helped Dance lower Ory to the ground. They carried Ory into the coach. Dance hastily bandaged the wound with his bandanna while Alec and Denny stood guard, watching the empty road behind them.

"Here they come!" screamed Denny. A knot of painted horsemen swept around a curve and toward the coach. Denny jumped inside the coach and slammed the door shut. Alec just made it to the shotgun messenger's seat as Dance lashed the team into a dead run.

Alec turned. He sighted on the leading warrior and opened fire. His third shot struck the horse, and the warrior was pitched over the mount's head. The other warriors streamed past the downed Tonto.

Alec saw a familiar horned headdress on one of the foremost warriors. It was almost impossible to sight from the pitching coach top, but he held as closely as he could and fired twice. The second slug struck Diabolito. He threw up his arms and fell sideways.

"I got Diabolito!" yelled Alec.

A slug whipped through the slack of his jacket. Another slug ripped a long splinter from the coach top and drove the end of it through Alec's left forearm. He clutched the Spencer with his left hand and ripped the splinter-free with his right hand. Blood trickled down into his palm.

"Bad?" called Dance.

"A scratch."

Dance stood up in the boot and flicked out his twelve-foot lash. "Two of the horses are wounded," he yelled. "Thanks to God, none of them was dropped."

The warriors fell behind, half hidden by the wreathing dust. Dance looked back over his shoulder and then slowed the spent team. "They haven't much left in them," said Dance. "Poor beggars. But they saved our lives."

Alec reloaded. He sat down and tied his bandanna about his wound. It hurt like fury, but it was no more than a flesh wound.

Dance drove for two more miles and then stopped the blown team. He dropped to the ground and looked under the coach. "Bad crack in the running gear," he said. "Watch for the Tontos, kid."

Dance wrapped a thong about the cracked running-gear member and then drew it tight. He wet it and then drank deeply from his canteen. He looked up at Alec. "Thanks, Alec," he said. "I was afraid I'd lose Ory over the side, and you know what they would have done to him if they had captured him."

Alec nodded.

Dance looked ahead. "We'll make Lone Hill soon," he said.

"Supposing the Tontos have been there?"

Dance wiped his face. "I told you once not to forecast things like that."

"I'm sorry."

"Forget it."

Denny looked out the window. "Ory is still unconscious, Dance. He's bleeding bad."

"Wrap more cloth over his wound. There's nothing else you can do."

Dance walked up and down the line of horses. "Poor beggars," he said again. Blood streamed down the rump of the nigh swing horse. The off-wheeler had a bullet gouge along his neck.

Dance swung up on his seat and released the brake. He walked the team. Alec looked back. The dust had settled on the road. There was no sign of the Tontos. It had been a close shave—*much too close.*

They passed Cuchillo Peak at last and began the

long descent from the ridge down toward the flats. Lone Hill station was hidden from them by a huge fold of the desert. There was no sign of smoke against the clear sky.

There was a thread of dust rising far behind the Concord.

"Dust behind," said Alec quietly.

"We'll make it to the station ahead of them," said Dance confidently.

"Yen."

Dance looked quickly at Alec, opened his mouth, and then shut it. He spoke to the team.

"I never lashed a team like that as long as I've been driving," said Dance. "This team is through as a Concord team. They'll never be any good for it again."

Alec closed his eyes against the dust. It was fifteen miles from Lone Hill to Tres Cabezas, and if there wasn't a fresh team at Lone Hill, the present team would never make it to the end of the line. If the Tontos caught the coach out in the open with a blown team, it would be the end for all of them.

"What time is it?" asked Alec as he opened his eyes.

"My watch is in my jacket pocket on your side."

Alec took out the watch and snapped open the lid. He shut the lid and put the watch back into Dance's pocket.

"Well?" asked Dance.

"Ten after two."

"Not too bad then."

"We can't make Tres Cabezas in time now."

"My watch is at least fifteen minutes fast."

"Even so, Dance!"

Dance looked calmly at Alec. "We're not going to quit, are we?"

Alec flushed. "Certainly not! But if we don't make the deadline, I don't think I'll be able to stand looking at Ross Corson's grinning face."

Dance spoke to the team and then looked at Alec again. "We won't have to, Alec."

The coach was at the top of the huge fold in the desert. Dance pointed with his whip. "There's Lone Hill."

Lone Hill rose from the flat desert floor. It was probably of volcanic origin, because it was composed of blackish rock with great winding gullies riven into its sides.

"The old blockhouse is on the far side," said Dance.

No smoke stained the clear sky. Alec looked back across the coach top. The dust was thicker now, and Alec saw a flash as if the sun had been reflected from something shiny.

"Getting any closer?" asked Dance.

"It seems like it, Dance."

The Concord neared Lone Hill. Dance looked back over his shoulder and touched up the team a little. Yellowish foam spattered from the horses' mouths, and their dusty flanks were streaked with sweat.

Then the blockhouse appeared, situated on a level place that was surrounded by great heaps of volcanic rock. There was a corral behind the blockhouse, but there wasn't a horse in sight. Alec felt his heart sink. This was the end, then, and the exhausted team could go no farther. A fresh team would have hauled the Concord into Tres Cabezas well ahead of the Tontos. Now, the only thing they could do was to hole up in the blockhouse until the Tontos returned to their hills.

Dance turned the team off the road and pulled up to the blockhouse. A rifle barrel showed for a moment through a loophole and then was hastily withdrawn. In a moment, the thick door creaked open on protesting hinges, and Bartolome Madera appeared, trailing a rifle.

"I did not expect to see you, Dance," said Bartolome. "The Tontos are on the warpath. We have stayed close to the blockhouse."

Two other King Line employees came out and looked curiously at the bullet-scarred coach.

Dance dropped from his seat and opened the coach door. Alec and Denny helped him take Ory Carter from the coach and carry him toward the blockhouse.

Dance looked at Alec. "This is the end, then," he said quietly. "No horses here."

Bartolome laughed. "We have a team, Dance," he said. "We were afraid the Tontos would run off our horses, so we took them into the blockhouse for safe-keeping."

"Yippee!" yelled Denny.

They carried Ory into the house. Bartolome and his men led the horses out of the blockhouse and harnessed them to the Concord. The sweat-lathered old team was taken inside.

Dance picked up a coil of wire and some heavy pliers and went to the coach. The men lifted up on the coach while Dance re-enforced his other lashings with the heavy wire. He checked the wheels and the running gear. He shook his head a little. "We'll probably make Tres Cabezas all right," he said, "but this coach won't be of much use after that. She's taken a terrible beating."

One of the swing station hostlers climbed up the slope. "There is dust out on the desert west of here. It looks like the Tontos are riding ahead to get in between you and the town."

Bartolome paled beneath his tan. "Then you cannot go on, Dance. They will shoot at the horses and then finish you off when the coach is stopped."

Dance wiped his hands. He threw the pliers and the wire into the coach. "We'll fox them," he said.

"How?" asked Alec.

"Let them go ahead. The road passes the Cone Hills about two miles north of here. There is a trail that leads to the east on this side of the Cone Hills. We'll take that trail to the east side of the hills and pick up the old Spanish Road. It will take us into Tres Cabezas. It's a little longer, of course, but we have no other choice."

"You won't make it on the old *camino*," protested Bartolome. "It has not been used for many years. It is full of holes and there are places where it disappears entirely."

"It's a chance we have to take," said Dance. "You boys can go along or stay here."

Alec climbed to his seat. Denny looked longingly at the solid blockhouse and then got into the coach. He picked up Ory's Spencer and settled himself into a seat. Dance grinned as he walked to the coach and mounted to his seat. He drove out onto the road.

Chapter Seventeen

THE TONTOS HAD A GOOD LEAD ON THE coach. Dance drove steadily until they neared the Cone Hills, a series of rounded hills looking like mounds of pudding. Dust drifted up far beyond the road. The Tontos were far ahead now, riding hard to close the trap. Dance searched the ground with his eyes and then he pointed with his whip. "There's the trail," he said.

Alec stared at it. It was hardly more than two faint ruts on the hard surface of the desert. There was no chance of going any other way, for the desert here was littered with rocks and gouged with gullies. Alec looked to the east. The trail followed the edge of the hills. At least they would be shielded from the eyes of the Tontos.

Dance turned the team onto the old trail. The Concord bumped over some small rocks. Dance drove at a steady mile-eating pace.

"Faster," pleaded Alec.

"No. We'll raise too much dust, and they might see it. Then they'd parallel us on the north side of the hills and meet us on the *camino*."

The sun was beating down, and the heat of it seemed to cut like a saber across the back of Alec's neck. His mouth tasted of dust. The metal of his carbine burned against his hands.

Dance drove carefully, for the old trail was no bargain as a road. Now and then, they reached deep gullies that cut across it, and the Concord seemed to protest in every joint as it bounced across them.

There was no sign of life on the flats or on the sunbaked Cone Hills. Time ticked on relentlessly as they rolled along below the hills. It seemed to Alec as if they'd never reach the end of them.

"The Old Spanish Road is about a mile ahead," said Dance.

Alec stood up and looked ahead. There was no sign of a road at first, and then he saw a faint line that seemed to cut through the mesquite and sage bushes. It must be the *camino*.

Dance darted a glance behind them. "No dust," he said.

The old road opened up before them. Dance turned the team to the north. The road was as Bartolome had said. It was full of holes and littered with rocks. Brush had taken hold here and there.

"It isn't much," said Dance cheerfully, "but it's better than the desert."

"Or meeting the Tontos."

"Roll her, Dance!" shouted Denny from below.

The Concord bounced from one chuckhole to another like a cockleshell on a choppy sea. Now and then, the wheels banged against rocks.

The Cone Hills were to the west. The *camino* trended away from them out into the rough desert, and for a time, Alec thought the road would never turn back, but when they were about two-thirds of the way past the hills, the road swung back again in a great arc. Then suddenly, there was no road at all. There was a great expanse of dried silt and sand, studded with stones and rocks as if there had been a flood through the area at one time.

Dance stopped the coach and stood up to look ahead. "Can you see the road?" he asked Alec.

Alec slanted his hat across his eyes and looked beyond the sandy area. A line of thick brush showed on the far side. "No," said Alec.

"I don't like the looks of that sand."

Alec nodded. Then he remembered a trick his father had once taught him on how to find a trail in the woods. He half closed his eyes and looked quickly from left to right and then back again. Suddenly, he saw a barely perceptible break in the line of brush. "There it is," he said to Dance.

"You've got eyes like an eagle."

"It's almost in line with that slab of yellowish rock."

Dance drove out on the sand, and immediately the wheels sank deeply into it. The horses strained against their collars. Alec dropped to the ground to lighten the load, and Denny jumped out beside him.

They slogged across the burning sand behind the laboring coach, shoving their shoulders against the rear thoroughbrace supports now and then to help the team. The sand seemed to burn clean through their boot soles.

Slower and slower went the coach until, at last, it bogged down completely. It took time to work the coach out. Then it went on again until, at last, they reached the far side of the big sand drift.

The road opened a way into the thick brush. The brush was higher than Alec's head, and the road seemed to vanish ahead of them at times, only to reappear again as the team plowed through brush that had sprouted on the old road.

Dance looked ahead. "We're almost at the end of the hills," he said. "I hope those Tontos are still waiting for us on the far side. I'd hate to see them show up now. We'd never outrun them on this road."

At the edge of the brush patch Dance let the team rest. Alec checked the running gear and thoroughbraces. The thongs and wire had been strained and stretched, and Alec was doubtful whether the thoroughbrace would hold up against any further punishment, but he did not want to worry Dance.

"How is it?" asked Dance.

"All right."

"Time's awastin'."

They climbed to their seats, and the coach rolled on. Alec was beginning to think they might make it yet. He glanced at the hazy hills shimmering in the heat. He started as he thought he saw a flash of light.

Alec stared at the barren hills until his eyes ached from the strain, but he did not see another flash. Perhaps it was his imagination, or the sun had sparkled from a piece of mica or quartz.

They reached the end of the hills, and the road turned west to follow along the base of the hills for a time. Alec was almost afraid to look at the heights for fear of what he might see, but he forced himself to do so at intervals.

Dance glanced at Alec. Suddenly, he began to sing:

> "Creeping through the valley, crawling o'er the
>   hill,
> Splashing through the branches, rumbling o'er
>   the mill,
> Putting nervous gentlemen in a towering
>   rage.
> What is so provoking as riding in a stage?"

Alec smiled. Dance always seemed to have an answer for everything.

"Alec," said Dance. "did you ever stop to think of how many travelers there were on this old *camino* in the days of its glory? Mule trains and *conductas* of silver from the mines near Tres Cabezas. Soldiers with polished helmets and bright breastplates. Priests spreading the word of God to the heathen Indians. Dark-eyed *señoritas* and fat *señoras*. Scouts and hunters. Prospectors and traders. I wish the old *camino* could talk to us."

"I wish the old *camino* would end."

Dance looked ahead. "No sign of dust. We're going to make it, Alec, my boy."

The road dipped down into a wide swale and then crossed an expanse of pebbles. As it rose to crest the slopes, Alec glanced at the hills. He saw another flash, and this time, he knew it wasn't the sun's reflection from quartz or mica. Alec knew now that it was a mirror flashing a message to someone down on the desert ahead of the Concord.

Alec shifted his Spencer and eased open the breech to see if a cartridge was in the chamber.

Dance began to sing again:

> *"Spinster fair and forty, maids in youthful*
> *   charms,*
> *Suddenly are cast into their neighbor's arms,*
> *Children shoot like squirrels darting through a*
> *   cage—*
> *sn't it delightful, riding in a stage?"*

Alec snapped shut the carbine breech.

"There's dust ahead of us, Dance," he said quietly.

"So there is."

Alec hung over the side of his seat. "Look alive, Denny!" he called.

"I ain't been doing anything else since we left Tonto Pass, Alec!" yelled back Denny.

"There's the Tres Cabezas road," said Dance.

The dust threaded up from the brush beyond the Tres Cabezas road. Then Alec saw three men riding hard toward the road. They were white men, but they had bound bandannas across their faces, and their hat brims were pulled low over their eyes. The sun glinted on the weapons in their hands.

Dance spoke sharply to the team and snapped his long lash over the heads of the leaders. The Concord reached the road two hundred yards ahead of the swiftly moving horsemen. Alec crawled atop the coach and hooked his boot toes under the rails. He rested his elbows on the coach top and snapped up the rear sight of his Spencer.

The coach was making fast time, but the horsemen were gaining a little. Dance kept on talking to the team. Alec heard a crackling noise from underneath the coach, above the rumbling of the wheels, the thud of hoofs, and the clucking of the sandboxes.

One of the pursuing horsemen fired. Alec did not answer the shot. A gun cracked again, and the slug rapped into the rear of the coach.

There was a startled cry from Denny Morris. "That was too close for comfort!" he bawled.

Alec fired over the heads of the three horsemen, hoping they would fall back, but they were too clever for him. They parted, and one of them stayed on the road while the other two separated. One of them turned his horse east of the road and rode in a sweeping curve to try to get ahead of the coach while the other did the same to the west.

Alec nodded grimly. His father had told him about the tactics of the Plains Indians who used the crescent running attack, such as the three men were trying now. The pursuit would be kept up by the rear party while two other parties forged ahead on the flanks, out of accurate shooting range, to creep up on the horses to try to down one or more of them and stop the coach. It was also a system used by Indians to run rabbits down on foot, with the rear runner keeping the rabbit moving while the two wing runners cut in steadily toward the frightened rabbit to make him run back and forth and cover more ground than his pursuers, and thus wear him out.

Alec pulled his hat low over his eyes. The riders in the Concord weren't frightened rabbits by a long shot. But Alec knew that the average white man was a far better shot than the average Indian, and the three pursuing men looked as if they could handle their weapons with skill.

Dance did not look back. He was relying on Alec to hold off the pursuit while Dance did his magic with reins, voice, and whip.

Denny fired from inside the coach. Alec waited until he got the left-hand rider full in his sights and then he fired. The rider seemed to wince a little, but his swift chase did not slow down.

The rear rider dropped his reins and raised his carbine. The sun glistened on the brass breech. It wasn't a repeater he was firing. It was a single-shot carbine. "A Burnside!" said Alec aloud just as the carbine spat flame and smoke. The slug hummed past Alec. The man was a fine shot.

Alec peppered out a few rounds but had no luck. Shooting was almost impossible on the swaying top of the racing coach. The rear rider reloaded swiftly. A gun cracked from the right-hand rider, and a horse whinnied sharply.

"Shoot for their horses, Alec!" yelled Dance.

Alec didn't want to do it. He hated the thought of killing the animals, but then he realized that their pursuers didn't have any such qualms about shooting the fine coach horses.

Alec fired at the left-hand rider's horse. The bay horse went down heavily, throwing its rider ahead of him.

The Burnside flashed again. Dance grunted in pain. Alec turned. Blood began to soak through Dance's buckskin jacket high on the left shoulder. Dance's left arm dropped, and the team felt the release of rein pressure.

The team turned a little to the right, and the coach wheels bounced and thudded on the rough shoulder of the road. Dance turned and shot a desperate look at Alec. "Take over, kid," he said between set teeth.

Alec crawled to the front of the coach and slid his carbine down between the two seats. Dance stood up. His hat blew off as he handed the reins to Alec. Alec immediately felt the powerful pressure of the running team.

Dance freed his Colt and began to fire deliberately. The right-hand rider fell back. A slug sang thinly as it glanced from a metal coach fitting.

Alec looked ahead. In the distance, below rugged hills, he could see smoke rising. On the hills were tall wooden structures. They were mine heads, he was sure.

"Tres Cabezas!" yelled Dance as he clumsily reloaded his smoking Colt.

The coach was now careening over hard flats that were as smooth as a billiard table. Alec turned the team from the rutted road and drove it onto the flats. He could hear Denny firing now and then from inside the coach.

The town was a mile and a half ahead, then a mile. Buildings began to show distinctly.

"Five minutes left!" yelled Dance. "Roll this swift-wagon, Alec!"

Half a mile from the town, there was a sharp cracking noise like a pistol shot. The coach jolted heavily. The weakened thoroughbrace was letting go. The coach tilted.

"She's resting on the brake beam, kid!" roared Dance. "Drive! Drive! Drive!"

Alec snapped the lash over the heads of the gallant leaders. Foam splattered back on Alec and Dance.

Alec dared to look back. The two remaining pursuers were far back in the billowing dust. The coach wallowed down into a dry wash, swayed sickeningly for a moment, and then righted itself again. It took the far bank of the wash with outraged creaking and groaning from the overburdened brake beam and running gear.

They thundered over the bridge spanning a dry creek and passed the outlying buildings of the town. A whisker of steam showed on a tall stack that towered over a mine building. Men stared at the sagging, careening Concord.

Alec stood up in the boot and swung his lash until his arm ached. The Concord slewed around a corner. The main street opened out in front of them. There was a faint noise from the big whistle on the mine stack.

The coach sagged still farther. Alec tooled the team to the right to avoid a heavily laden ore wagon. They shot past it with inches to spare, and the angry shout of the driver followed them.

Alec saw the frame shack that housed the King Line office. A freshly painted sign hung out in front of it. The big whistle screamed into life, echoing from the dun hills.

The brake beam snapped like a gunshot. The coach slewed and then crashed heavily full into the front-of-the-line office. Dance leaped from his seat like a great ungainly bird and landed, spraddle-legged, in the street. There was a muffled cry from Denny Morris. Alec dropped the reins and slid to the ground. Glass from the broken office window crunched beneath his boots.

Stewart Ellis, the office manager, pushed open the office door and stared at the sweat-lathered rump of a wheelhorse inches from his face. He looked up and down the crashed coach and then at Dance and Alec. "You always end a run like this? It'll cost the company more money to repair the office than you'll make on the mail contract."

Dance gripped his shoulder and managed a painful grin. "That was the four o'clock whistle from the Good Luck Mine, wasn't it?"

Ellis nodded.

"Then we made the run in time," said Dance, "and saved the mail franchise."

"What a way to do it!" said Ellis as he shook his head.

A crowd gathered about the wrecked coach. Dance gripped the arm of a big miner. "Get the deputy sheriff," he said. "We were jumped by road agents this side of Cone Hills."

The miner ran down the dusty street.

Stewart Ellis walked about the coach. A mailbag sailed from the coach window and hit him on the head. He staggered back and was hit by another one. The dust-covered face of Denny Morris showed at the window. The sun shone on his tousled red hair. "There's your mail," said Denny with a wide grin.

"Get a doctor for Dance," said Alec. "He's been shot."

Two men helped Dance into the office. Others unhitched the blown team and led it off. Alec leaned against the office front. Reaction had set in after the hazardous drive. Denny crawled from the coach and dragged the heavy payroll chest out after him. He sat on it and placed his carbine across his lap. "You can tell the mine manager his payroll is here," he said to a red-shirted miner.

"I'll take it to him," said the miner.

"You will not," said Denny firmly. "This is the responsibility of the King Line. I'll sit on this chest until we get a receipt from the mine manager."

The miner laughed. "If the King Line has two kids

bringing in their coaches and payroll consignments," he said. "I'd like to see what kind of *men* they have working for them."

———

LATER, after Dance's wound had been probed and the bullet removed from the wound, the driver fingered the extracted slug. "Another Burnside," he said quietly. "Did you recognize any of those road agents, Alec?"

"It was too dusty, and I wasn't trying to recognize any of them. I was too excited, I guess."

Dance nodded. He looked at Stewart Ellis. "Has Ross Corson been seen in Tres Cabezas?"

"Not lately."

"I didn't think he would be."

"Do you think he had anything to do with your troubles on the road?"

"I don't know. But Corson was out in those hills somewhere and so were Rig Conboy and Monk Dorn. The Tontos raided Tonto Pass station and wiped it out. The Tontos have been getting new repeating rifles from somewhere, and Monk Dorn has a reputation as a gunrunner."

Ellis paled. "Then we'll have plenty of trouble from now on."

Dance shook his head. "I'm going to run those wolves to earth," he said.

The doctor placed a hand on Dance's bandaged

shoulder. "You'll have to take it easy for a time," he said.

"I haven't got time. I've been shot before and may get shot again, but I'm going to find out if those three men are the renegades I think they are."

"Let's eat," said Denny.

Dance grinned. "On me. Let's go, boys. Our work isn't through yet."

Alec nodded. "We saved the King Line anyway," he said.

"You two men did most of the work," said Dance.

Denny smiled at Alec. "Now, maybe your pa will give me a job," he said.

They walked out into the bright sunlight.

Chapter Eighteen

ALEC STOOD AT THE WINDOW OF THE HOTEL room, looking down upon the lamplit main street of Tres Cabezas. The street was crowded with miners who had finished their shifts. A piano tinkled from somewhere down the street. Alec started as he saw a familiar man standing across the street. It was Ross Corson.

Stewart Ellis was talking to Dance Birney while Denny Morris lay on a bed digging into a huge bag of hard candy.

"The posse found Monk Dorn beside the road," he said. "His right arm and collarbone were broken, and he was out of his mind. He couldn't or wouldn't talk, but we figured he was the man Alec downed. We couldn't find a trace of the other two road agents."

"I'd be willing to bet they were Ross Corson and Rig Conboy," said Dance.

"Be careful," warned Stewart. "Those two men are

dangerous. They won't stand for any loose talk about them."

Alec turned. "Ross Corson is across the street," he said.

The two men came to the window and looked down at Corson. "It's him all right," said Dance.

Stewart Ellis nodded. "What do you intend to do now?"

Dance turned to Denny. "Denny," he said, "go on down and nose about. Try to find out when Corson got into town."

Denny jumped to his feet. "That's my dish," he said.

"Don't make it too obvious, kid."

Denny laid a finger alongside his nose. "We Pinker-tons *never* make things look too obvious. We can't afford to."

Denny left the room. Alec looked down into the street, but Ross Corson was gone.

"T sent a messenger to Bert King," said Ellis. "A good man who can get past the Tontos if anyone can. He'll tell Bert what happened and get men out to Tonto Pass station to man it. Bert will want to get another coach through as soon as possible to begin the service on this division."

"The boys and I will leave here tomorrow and head back too."

"What about the Tontos?"

"We'll take a chance on that. They were after the coach and horses. Besides, the posse is patrolling between here and Lone Hill. The Tontos will lay low. They won't tangle with those boys."

Denny was back in half an hour. "Corson came into town about seven o'clock riding a fine black," he said breathlessly.

"Did you see his horse?"

"It's down at the livery."

"Did it look as if it had been ridden hard?"

"No."

"None of the men who chased us rode a black," said Alec.

"Doesn't mean anything," said Denny wisely. "Corson would have been too smart to ride a black that is well known to us."

"Yes, he would," said Dance. "I'd like to talk to Monk Dorn."

"I doubt if it will do any good," said Ellis.

"I can try."

The four of them left the room and walked to the jail. Monk Dorn was in a rear cell. The jailkeeper shook his head as they asked to see Monk. "He's just about gone," he said. "Internal injuries."

He led them to the cell and opened the door. Monk's eyes were closed. He opened them as Dance spoke to him. There was a glazed look in Monk's eyes. "Who was with you, Monk?" asked Dance.

"*Amigos.*"

"Who?"

Monk looked away. "Let me alone," he said.

"It'll go easier on you if you talk."

Monk laughed and then coughed harshly. "I don't squeal on my *amigos*," he said.

"Did you run guns into the Tontos?"

"What if I did? You can't do anything to me now."

"But you *did*."

"It's my business."

"Diabolito is dead."

"So?"

"You ran guns into his country. Did he get them?"

"Yes."

"Did you do it on your own?"

Monk shook his head. "I got good pay to do it."

"Rig Conboy and you left town together."

"Don't mean a thing."

"What did you do at Lopez Seep?"

Monk eyed Dance and then he closed his eyes.

"Nothing."

"Did Ross Corson pay you to take guns into the Tonto country to deliver to Diabolito?"

Monk breathed spasmodically, and then he lay still. The jailer felt Monk's pulse and then raised one of his eyelids. "He's gone," he said quietly.

Alec turned on a heel and left the jail. Dance came out behind Alec and placed a hand on his shoulder. "You had to do it. Alec," he said. "Think of what would have happened to us if they had stopped the coach."

"I don't like the thought of having killed a man."

"You killed his horse. The fall killed him."

"But I caused his death," cried Alec.

Dance roughly turned Alec. "Listen," he said

harshly. "If they had stopped us, do you think they would have let us live? We would have recognized them. They would have killed us right there."

Alec nodded. "I guess you're right."

"You know I am! Let's get some sleep."

Denny followed them to the hotel. "*I'm* not sorry about Monk Dorn," he said.

"You didn't kill him," said Alec shortly.

Alec lay awake for a long time, listening to the steady breathing of Denny Morris, who lay beside him. Alec walked to the window and looked down into the street.

"Forget it, Alec," said Dance from his bed. "I killed my first man when I was sixteen. He had killed a Mexican kid for no reason at all. Then he went after me. I *had* to kill him, or he would have killed me. An eye for an eye, Alec."

Alec went back to bed and got in. Dance was right. Kill or be killed. He went to sleep right away.

They reached Lone Hill late in the morning, as they brought a six-horse team with them for the station. Bartolome Madera told them that not a Tonto had been seen since the coach had passed through. Ory Carter was well but decided to stay at the station until the next coach came through, and then he would ride in it to Cabezas to have a doctor inspect his wound.

They made Tonto Pass at dusk. Marty Roe, Denny's uncle, had come out from Yucca Plats to take charge of the home station. Freshly mounded graves showed on a low hill to the north of the fort. Marty was angry at Denny, but Dance talked him out of giving the kid a good scolding.

By noon the next day, the trio had reached Stony Creek, and there they met the upcoming coach driven by Slim Pastor, with KirbyTodd riding as shotgun messenger. There were four passengers, all heavily armed, in the Concord.

"Any sign of 'Paches?" Slim asked Dance.

"None."

"I ain't worried. The six of us can take care of ourselves."

The trio watched the Concord start out on its trip to Tonto Pass and then they continued on their journey to Cactus Spring. They spent the night there, and the next morning, went on to Yucca Flats.

Bert King didn't have much to say to them when they reached his office, but his gratitude was plain to see. Alec was surprised that his father didn't rawhide him, but evidently, the courier Stewart Ellis had sent on ahead had talked considerably about what Denny and Alec had done to see that the first run on the new road was a success.

Dance told Bert of his suspicions of Rig Conboy and Ross Corson. Bert nodded. "Rig Conboy showed up here yesterday," he said, "but no one has seen Ross Corson since he left here for Tres Cabezas."

Alec's father walked to his wall map and drew blue lines over the red ones he had drawn to show the new division. "I've got twenty reservations for the next week," he said. "Also, a lot of express shipments. The mining company has contracted with me to deliver their payrolls every two weeks. It looks good. Dance."

"There's still the matter of who killed Charley Lee and who robbed the mails in Owl Pass. It was Rig Conboy, I'm sure."

"Fred Horton hasn't preferred charges against Rig Conboy as yet. He's waiting for more evidence."

Denny grinned. "I'll find it," he said.

"You'll go home and make peace with your father and mother, young man," ordered Bert King.

Denny hastily left the office and sped up the street.

Alec's father looked through the window at his destroyed wagon shed and stables. "Jonas Miller left town," he said. "The man was badly frightened about something. He'd been doing some loose talking about town."

"About what?" asked Dance.

"Something about knowing quite a bit about that fire."

"So?"

"It seems that he was given some money to stay away from his night watchman job that night."

"I had a feeling there was dirty work done that night."

"They say he's staying in Junction, afraid to come back here."

Dance slapped the dust from his clothing. "Alec, you and I better get cleaned up and get something to eat. After that, I'll go into Junction and see Jonas."

Bert King shrugged. "I want you to look at some

new horses I bought first. Besides, I doubt if you'll learn anything from Jonas."

"We'll see."

"Can I go along with you, Dance?" asked Alec. "Jonas always liked me."

"That's true," said Alec's father. "But be careful."

"Of Jonas?" Dance laughed.

"It isn't Jonas I'm warning you about. Whoever paid him that money to keep quiet will try to see to it that he keeps his big mouth shut."

Dance nodded. "Yes. I see what you mean."

Dance and Alec left the office and went home to clean up and get fresh clothing.

———

IT WAS dusk when Alec and Dance reached Junction, for Bert King, as always, had valued Dance's opinion on the stock he had bought.

"I wonder where we'll find Jonas," said Dance.

"We'll ask at Cahan's Store. There isn't much going on around here that Mr. Cahan doesn't know."

Cahan told them Jonas was living in a rundown jacal at the edge of town. They rode to it. Light showed from the lone window. Dance swung down and eased his Colt into its holster. He looked in through the window and nodded. Dance walked to the door and kicked it open. Jonas looked up from his cot. "What's the idea?" he demanded.

Alec came into the filthy room and shut the door

behind him. Dance leaned against the wall. "We've missed you in Yucca Flats, Jonas," he said quietly.

"Yeh? You ain't even been there lately."

"Why did you leave town, Jonas?"

Jonas looked away. "No one would give me a job because of my leaving my post as watchman the night of the big fire," he said sourly.

"Why *did* you leave your post?"

"I was cold."

Dance nodded. He looked about the littered room. "Maybe I can talk Bert King into giving you a job out at one of the new stations," he said.

Jonas rose to the bait. "You will?"

"I will if you'll tell me who paid you to leave your post."

Jonas paled. "I didn't say I was paid."

"No, you didn't."

Jonas got up and came close to Dance. "If I told, I might not live to work for Bert," he said quietly.

Alec was near the door. He thought he heard faint footsteps outside.

"Who paid you?" demanded Dance of Jonas.

Jonas wet his thin lips. "Rig Conboy," he said.

"Did he start the fire?"

"I—" Jonas's voice was cut off by the smashing of glass as the shattered window splattered Alec. A rifle muzzle was thrust through the window. Alec gripped it and thrust it upward. The gun roared, and the slug struck the ceiling. Dance swept the lamp from the table. Jonas shrieked and tore open the rear door. He bounded through it and ran screaming toward the brushy creek bottoms.

Alec dropped to the floor and jerked at the rifle. It came free in his hands. There was a muttered exclamation outside the jacal and then the thud of boots striking the hard ground. Then they heard the rapid tattoo of hoofs. Dance tore open the front door and ripped out his Colt. He fired twice at the racing horseman, but the man turned his horse into the trees that bordered the road and was gone from sight.

The room stank of gunpowder mingled with the fumes of the smashed lamp. Dance lighted a match and found a candle. Alec looked at the weapon in his hands. It was a sure-enough Burnside with a brass breech. Alec looked at Dance. Dance took the carbine and looked at the breech. "R.C," he said as he traced the engraved initials on the breech. "Rig Conboy, or I'm a Tonto. Come on, Alec! We've got work to do!" They rode swiftly for Yucca Flats.

Chapter Nineteen

BERT KING LISTENED QUIETLY TO DANCE'S story. He put on his hat and buckled his gun belt about his waist. "Let's pay a visit to Rig Conboy," he said.

Alec started for the door with the two men. His father shook his head. "Go on home, Son," he said. "This is up to Dance and myself."

Alec stood in the street and watched them walk toward the hotel. He led Biscuits up the street to the house and then tethered the horse to the picket fence. He sat down on the front porch, with his heart in his mouth. Rig Conboy was a violent and dangerous man.

There was a soft whistle from the shadows. Denny Morris limped into Alec's view. "Man, oh man," he said. "Did I get it!"

"Sit down, Denny."

Denny shook his head ruefully. "Not tonight," he said.

Two horsemen appeared on the road. Denny drew in his breath. "Look!" he hissed.

They were Rig Conboy and Ross Corson.

Alec sped to Biscuits and jerked his Sharps from its scabbard. He raced through the brush and jumped behind a tree. Denny came up behind him. "You ain't going to try and stop them, are you, Alec?"

Alec cocked and capped his carbine. "I'm not going to *try* to stop them," he said. "I'm *going* to stop them."

Denny slipped Alec's little Colt from its holster. "Okay, okay," he said. "I'll stick with you."

The two men were fifty feet away. Alec stepped out into the moonlight and raised his Sharps. "Stop where you are," he said.

"It's that King kid," said Rig.

Ross Corson drew in his horse. "Get out of the way," he said coldly to Alec.

"Get off those horses."

"Sure. Sure," said Rig. He slid from his horse and looked at Alec with a smile. "What's on your mind, kid? Playing road agent? You should oughta be in bed."

Denny Morris moved through the brush and came out on the road behind the two men.

"Another one," said Rig.

Ross Corson folded his arms. "Put away that carbine," he said to Alec.

Alec shook his head. "You've got some talking to do," he said. "Denny! Go get my father and Dance."

Denny sped off down the moonlit road.

Ross Corson faced Alec. "You've only got one shot

in that piece of junk," he said. "Even if you do get one of us, the other one will get you, kid. Get out of the way!"

Alec gripped his Sharps. "Don't try anything," he said.

Rig grinned. "Come on now. You don't want to get hurt. Sonny."

"You've got some explaining to do."

"About what?"

"You'll find out. Keep those hands up! Walk ahead of me back toward my house."

The two men walked slowly, glancing back over their shoulders at Alec. They whispered to each other.

When they reached the house, Alec was relieved to see Dance Birney and Bert King running toward them. Denny Morris manfully brought up the rear.

Ross Corson suddenly whirled. His hand snaked inside his coat and then whipped out with a short-barreled pistol in it. Alec fired. The flash and smoke of the gun startled Corson. He jumped to one side and fired. The slug rapped into a tree.

Rig Conboy ran for his horse. Alec threw his Sharps between Conboy's legs, and he fell heavily.

Dance drew his Colt. Corson turned. Dance fired once and Corson winced, but he raised his Colt as Bert King moved in. Bert swung his pistol hard against Corson's head. The stage line owner went down on his knees, dropping his Colt.

Dance ran to Conboy. As the big man got to his feet, Dance hit him with his gun barrel. Conboy went down again. Smoke hung over the scene as the two men were disarmed.

They marched Corson and Conboy back to the office and tied their hands. Bert King sat on the edge of his desk and looked steadily at them. "What was the big hurry in leaving town?" he asked.

"You've got nothing on me!" snapped Corson.

Rig Conboy turned to look at his boss.

"No?" asked Dance. "Who held up our coaches in Owl Pass? Who killed Charley Lee? Who fired the wagon shed and stables? Who set the Tontos against us? Who were the two men who were with Monk Dom when we were attacked just outside of Tres Cabezas?"

Corson wet his lips. "It was Conboy who held up the coaches in Owl Pass. He killed Charley Lee. He fired the wagon shed and stables. Monk Dom and Rig Conboy ran guns into the Tonto country for Diabolito's band."

Rig Conboy paled. "You skunk!" he said.

"It's true," said Corson.

"Yeh," sneered Conboy. "It was under your orders, Corson. You paid for the guns we ran into the Tonto country."

Dance gripped Conboy by the shirt front. "Who were the two men with Monk Dorn when the coach was attacked?"

"Keep your mouth shut!" yelled Corson.

Rig looked into Dance's cold eyes. "It was me and Corson," he said. "Look, Birney, if I turn state's evidence, will I get a break?"

"You killed Charley Lee."

"Corson said so."

"Did you?"

Conboy looked away. Dance shoved him into a seat. "Never mind," he said. "The law will sweat it out of you."

Corson held his head in his hands. Conboy looked from Dance to Bert and then to Alec and Denny. "I was only obeying orders," he said brokenly.

"Get the marshal, Denny," said Bert King quietly.

The marshal took the two prisoners to the jail. Alec, his father, Dance, and Denny watched them shamble up the street.

"It's all over," said Dance.

Bert King nodded. "I can't believe men would do things the way they did," he said.

"It's hard to believe," agreed Dance.

Alec's father put out the light, and the four of them left the office. "Let's go to the house," said Bert King. "I've got some prime steaks there. This calls for a celebration."

They walked up the street. "What do I owe you, Alec?" asked his father.

"Nothing."

"There must be *something* you want."

"Hit him for a job for me," urged Denny.

Bert King smiled. "What would you like to have, Denny?" he asked.

"A job on the King Line."

Bert nodded. "In time," he said. "Denny, you've

got brains. You finish your schooling and then you'll get your job."

"I was afraid you'd say that. Mr. King."

Alec looked at Dance Birney. The coach driver smiled at him. "What about Dance?" asked Alec.

Alec's father waved a hand. "I need a new division manager," he said. "That man is Dance Birney. I can't think of a better man to supervise the Tres Cabezas Division."

"Amen to that," said Alec.

"I'll keep the swiftwagons rolling," promised Dance.

"We're playing a part in the development of this Territory," said Alec's father. "Someday, it will be a great state. In time, the railroads will take over from the stagecoach lines, and we'll be out of business, but it will be worth it."

Dance nodded. "You'll always make a living in transportation Bert," he said. "It's in the blood."

Alec looked up at the distant Grindstone Hills, bathed in soft silvery moonlight. Men had fought and died to get the line through to Tres Cabezas—unsung heroes of American transportation. He was proud to have been a part of the hard struggle.

It was a clear fall day in October of 1878 as the swift Concord reached the top of Tonto Pass. Alec King reined the six-horse team to a halt in front of Tonto Pass home station. He set the brake and wound the reins around the brake handle. "Ho, greasers!" he called out.

The greasers ran out with their pots and brushes

to slake hot hubs and axles. Hostlers trotted out the sprightly fresh team. Marty Roe came from the station and grinned up at Alec and Dance Birney. "Inspection trip?" he asked.

Dance Birney, Division Manager for the Tres Cabezas Division of King Lines, nodded. "How does it go, Marty?"

"Fine." Marty eyed Alec. "Who's the man with you, Dance? Seems to me his face is right familiar. Reminds me of that kid, Alec King, who was such a pest five years ago."

Alec grinned. "The very same," he said.

"How are you, Alec? How's college?"

"I'm fine, Marty. I'm skipping this semester to come here and work for Dad."

"¡Bueno!"

Alec looked at the big station. It didn't seem as if five years had passed since he had seen the station burning from the Tonto raid. He looked at the grass-mounded graves on the slope beyond the station.

They moved out quickly for the run to Lone Hill, with Alec up on the driver's box, driving the fast-moving team. Denny Morris was a Wells Fargo special agent now in Tres Cabezas, and Alec was looking forward to seeing him. The King Line now included the old Corson Line division to Fort Ireland and beyond. Ross Corson was still serving time in Yuma Penitentiary, while Rig Conboy had paid the extreme penalty for the murder of Charley Lee.

"Hiyup! Hi! Hi! G'lang! G'lang there!" called Alec to the team.

Dance leaned back in his seat. "You haven't forgotten how to tool a Concord," he said.

"I had a good teacher. Dance."

"Your dad has plans for you," said Dance. "He's bought out Park and Company Freighting Line."

Alec nodded as he drove the team around a sharp curve.

Dance slanted his hat across his eyes. "Somehow, I miss the old days."

"The Southern Pacific Railroad has reached the Colorado at Yuma," said Alec. "In time, they'll have branch lines all over Arizona Territory, Dance."

Dance nodded. "There is still a need for stage lines, and when the day comes when they are not needed, they'll still need freighting lines. There will always be a place for us. Alec."

The swiftwagon swayed and bobbed as the team forged on toward Lone Hill. The day of the Concord stagecoach would soon be over, but the swiftwagons had made pages of history in Arizona Territory as well as all over the West. They would never be forgotten.

"G'lang! Hi yup!" called out Alec. "Keep apulling! We've got to make Tres Cabezas on schedule! Hi yup! G'lang!"

A scarf of yellow dust hung in the pass as the swiftwagon rolled onto Tres Cabezas.

A Look At:

Son of the Thunder People and Tumbleweed Trigger

Award-winning author Gordon D. Shirreffs is known for his epics tales of the Wild West, each one more exhilarating than the last.

In *Son of the Thunder People*, fifteen-year-old Alan Warden is taken captive by the Chiricahuas, arguably the fiercest of all the Apache divisions. With the help of Never Still, Alan learns the language and the Apache ways, eventually becoming a blood brother and a medicine man—rather than a killer. But when an opportunity for deceit arises, will Alan choose to betray the Apache or honor them instead?

Tumbleweed Trigger follows Matt Turlock, a drifter and ne'er-do-well, who can't be depended upon to do anything useful —other than look out for his own hide. When Commander Jim Sturtevant asks Turlock to watch his back—and, if necessary, risk his life—the commander winds up dead. Will Turlock do the right thing and avenge his friend, or will his drifter ways pull him right into the ranks of the hired killers?

AVAILABLE NOW

About the Author

Gordon D. Shirreffs published more than 80 western novels, 20 of them juvenile books, and John Wayne bought his book title, Rio Bravo, during the 1950s for a motion picture, which Shirreffs said constituted *"the most money I ever earned for two words."* Four of his novels were adapted to motion pictures, and he wrote a Playhouse 90 and the Boots and Saddles TV series pilot in 1957.

A former pulp magazine writer, he survived the transition to western novels without undue trauma, earning the admiration of his peers along the way. The novelist saw life a bit cynically from the edge of his funny bone and described himself as looking like a slightly parboiled owl. Despite his multifarious quips, he was dead serious about the writing profession.

Gordon D. Shirreffs was the 1995 recipient of the Owen Wister Award, given by the Western Writers of America for "a living individual who has made an outstanding contribution to the American West."

He passed in 1996.

Made in the USA
Middletown, DE
27 June 2024

56480031R00120